T0193991

Paths *and* Places

Paths *and* Places

Riv Loomis

Paths and Places

iUniverse books may be ordered through booksellers or by contacting:

iUniverse
1663 Liberty Drive
Bloomington, IN 47403
www.iuniverse.com
1-800-Authors (1-800-288-4677)

ISBN: 978-1-4917-7188-4 (sc)
ISBN: 978-1-4917-7187-7 (e)

Library of Congress Control Number: 2015914068

Print information available on the last page.

iUniverse rev. date: 01/30/2016

Contents

Introduction..vii

Chapter 1   Directions 1

Chapter 2   Needed 9

Chapter 3   Stall... 13

Chapter 4   Garden Party.............................. 23

Chapter 5   Tea 30

Chapter 6   Stopping By 36

Chapter 7   Fresh Grass................................. 39

Chapter 8   Fingertip 44

Chapter 9   Delivery 49

Chapter 10   Ridge 54

Chapter 11   Hallway 57

Chapter 12   Relaxing....................................... 62

Chapter 13   New Place 65

Chapter 14   Workout 88

Chapter 15   Upstairs.. 94

Chapter 16   Blindfold...................................... 98

Chapter 17   Primal 110

Chapter 18   Drinks 121

Chapter 19   Together.. 125

Chapter 20   Behind 134

Chapter 21   After Work.................................... 141

Chapter 22   Lunch 149

Chapter 23 No Hurry.. 152
Chapter 24 Edged 155
Chapter 25 Holiday.. 168
Chapter 26 Chair 189
Chapter 27 Coupons... 197
Chapter 28 Bored.. 203
Chapter 29 Cubicle 207
Chapter 30 Waiting... 212
Chapter 31 Washcloth... 216
Chapter 32 Robe 218

Introduction

This book contains thirty-two short stories of romance erotica.

CHAPTER 1

Directions

It's been a long day. I told you I would be late getting home. You said *okay* and managed to hide your sigh of disappointment as I told you I would see you tonight and we hung up. Then came more patients and paperwork and craziness; sigh. Long day. You pull into the driveway, turn off the radio, and get out of your car, tired but wired, wanting something to do—wanting sex. You come up to the back door and let yourself in. The screen door closes behind you as you place your work stuff on the counter and exhale. Home, finally; maybe put on some music and have a glass of wine, maybe take a bubble bath. The dull yearning, tingling in your stomach, and the need for something in your pussy; you leave the kitchen and turn toward the living room and the stereo. Maybe some music and a little wine; maybe some quick play.

"Hi."

"Oh my God! What the—you're home! You scared the hell out of me, thank you very much."

"Well, you're always leaving for work early, and we always miss each other. I thought I'd change it up a little and come home from work early and surprise you."

"Surprise me … yeah."

I brush by you with a light touch on your shoulder and a quick kiss on your cheek. You turn and see me sitting comfortably in the recliner. The chair is fully up, and my arms are on the armrests, my hands down, fingertips tapping slowly. You stand there, leaning with your hand up on the archway. Our conversation pauses for a moment as we look into each other's eyes. You are noticing that I haven't made any effort to move, noticing my fingertips tapping idly and the way I'm looking at you. You open your mouth slightly and casually touch the tip of your tongue to your teeth. The silence between us gets longer, and the heat in the room rises as you stare back with a serious look, a look of waiting to see what I have in mind. My fingers tap once. Your sensual eyes are mesmerizing. I want to get up and take you right now.

"Baby, unbutton your blouse."

You touch the tip of your tongue to your lips for just a moment, continuing to look into my eyes as your hands come up and touch your blouse. Your hands come down as I watch the buttons undone; your blouse opening and hanging open and your bra visible. With the heat and the rising tension, your pulse quickens, and your body tightens with a need and expectation that makes you a little shaky as your hands go slowly down to your sides and you wait.

"Now the bra. You know I want to see those tits."

Calm and relaxed, my voice goes lower; the sharp sparkle of lust is clear in my eyes now. You bring your hands up again and open the clasp, your fingertips touching and easing the cups off. Your bra falls open, exposing your breasts. You haven't looked away, and your face is calm, even as you feel the air on your skin and how hard your nipples are, hard and pointing, throbbing and sensitive. Pinching fingers would feel, oh God, so fucking good. You see my fingertips tapping, and your pussy turns to a horny, wet mess as your hands go back down to your sides. Your breath comes out shallow from the very top of your chest.

"Now the pants."

My stare goes directly into your mind as you move your hands to the front of your slacks. Your fingertips touch on the waistband and the fabric; your hands feel slow and shaky, made clumsy by the horniness throbbing in your cunt. Your knees weak, and your need to fuck is almost overwhelming now.

"Go down … slide your fingers over … yes. Touch on it … rub now … yes. You were going to take a bath before I got home, weren't you? Maybe have a glass of wine … a little play?"

You are staring into my eyes as I speak; it's clearly taking some effort as you let out a shuddery gasp. Two fingers of your hand press and slide on their own, down and then back up, on the thin fabric directly over your pussy. You close your mouth and swallow before you give a quick nod and breathe out again, watching my growing lust for you slacken my face as I continue to look into your eyes.

"Legs apart … yes. Good girl. Rub … right there … yes. You are so beautiful when you're horny."

You shift your legs until they're shoulder-width apart, barely slowing your two fingers pressing and sliding on your crotch. I see you wanting to speed up, wanting to jam your fingers inside and frig your pussy to a hard cum, those almost-there-but-not-maddeningly-close fingers, pressing your pants and panties onto your dripping, swollen slit with a discreet vengeance that has your knees bending and straightening. The heat is visible on your face as you feel the dampness coming through. You keep your face calm and defiant, dismissive and self-respecting, even as you feel your panties shifting under your pressing fingers and feel the orgasm threatening to happen from deep in your spasming cunt.

"A nice, warm bubble bath … foamy bubbles … your hand going under the bubbles."

Your knees buckle and straighten; your hand presses flat on the archway as you bend forward into the coming orgasm. You stop yourself, barely in time, and straighten up, your breath catching and then hissing out. You don't know how much longer—

"Go ahead, baby … use both hands."

Your hand is down from the archway and joined with your other hand. *Oh God, thank you, sir*—

"No. Stop. Take your hands away."

You don't want to; you're too far now, and you can't stop. You won't stop.

"I said stop. Right now. Hands away."

The tone of my voice stays calm and understanding as I repeat the command to stop. Your eyes are tearing as you stare at me, before you look down and will your hands to stop, will your hands to move away; the obvious wet spot in your slacks. You feel the heat of embarrassment on your face, even as your whole body is begging you to continue. You get your hands to your sides finally and manage to look up, shaking and lusting and shook up and needy, biting on your lower lip and waiting.

"Undo the clasp … get that zipper down."

You look down hard with barely seeing eyes and get your hands up, finding and undoing the clasp and yank, pulling the zipper down, swallowing open-mouthed and breathing quick breaths. The zipper opens wide, and you see your soaked panties.

"Now pull your pants down."

You grab on at the sides and pull your slacks down to midthigh.

"Down to your knees … good girl … and now your panties."

You get your slacks down to your knees and remain bent over as you reach up for your panties, getting them down to your slacks before straightening up.

"Your panties are soaked. You must be very horny … yes?"

You glance into my eyes and nod. Not sure what you are thinking now … only the sound of my voice, low and calm and warm, sympathetic and firm.

"Take off your shirt … and your bra. Throw them over the chair."

Your blouse rests on the edge of the chair, and your bra lands close to it. With your panties at your knees and your slacks down around your ankles, you turn back around to face me. Otherwise naked, your nipples are hard, dark, throbbing raspberries, and your breasts are begging to be held, to be gripped. Your stomach is tight and fluttery, and you feel the wetness on the insides of your thighs, your swollen, overstimulated-to-the-edge-of-orgasm pussy. You stand there straight and waiting and shamelessly obedient on shaking legs.

"Come here."

You were expecting to be told to step out of your pants. You look at me for a moment before you begin to shuffle forward, awkward little baby steps. Your pussy lips rub together with each movement of your legs. You glance up at me, and the sudden wave of submissiveness that sweeps over you forces you to swallow hard, forces you to concentrate with all of your effort to get to me. The little-girl cuteness of your shuffling feet and your nakedness and your open submissiveness tightens the orgasmic knot in your pussy.

You feel lightheaded with the need to hide all of that from me; it's so embarrassing.

"Turn around for me."

You don't look up; the heat on your face is intense. You turn yourself away from me with mincing, shuffling steps. You almost jump as you feel my hands, sudden and gentle, on the cheeks of your ass.

"Bend."

Lightheaded and shaky and compliant, you begin to bend forward. At the same moment you feel my hands slide around to the front of your thighs and pull you back, you feel the sudden press of my face on the backs of your thighs and the masculine, probing tongue in your slit. You feel yourself squat, your ass cheeks spreading and your cunt fully offered. My hands are sure and strong and owning your legs, your pussy sucked on as you're tongue-fucked with an animal intensity that takes your breath away and puts you on the very edge of cumming. *It's all good, it's so good. Oh God, keep going, don't stop, don't stop—*

The tongue is gone suddenly, and the hands are gone, and you are standing facing away, about to cum, wanting to cum so badly, you can barely stand it. You hear the mechanical sounds of the recliner and then my words. "Step out of those clothes. Turn around."

Every muscle tight, you step out of your slacks and let your panties drop. You turn around to face me and see that I have eased the recliner back and am lying almost flat on my back. I stare into your eyes, whispering with a voice hoarse from tenderness, love, and lust. "Climb up here. Climb up and sit on my face."

Your blouse and bra are on the chair behind you, your slacks and panties in a pile beside your bare feet. You are looking at me and listening, barely believing how turned on you are as you stare at my face and mouth and listen. There is nowhere else you'd rather be. Your pussy is moving and dripping juices as my words and my gaze and your own most private, dirty thoughts converge. You're trembling now with a naked need for relief that allows only your sexual self to stand before me, taking in my voice and words. Moving forward, you reach the soft, black leather of the recliner and knee-step onto it. You look down and turn yourself carefully away from me, placing your foot down at my side and getting your other foot down. You feel my hands slide up gently, guiding your thighs, and you begin to sit back. Your weight shifts down to my raised hands, and you lower yourself. Your hands touch the armrests, and then you feel my lips meeting your pussy, my lips and tongue; the pleasure is sudden and explosive, and you give yourself up into my hands. You press your pussy down full on my face, on my cheeks and cheekbones, and my tongue up inside and moving around in circles. *Oh my fucking God, ohhh shit, ohhhh Jesus.*

Your back straightens, and your weight pushes your pussy down even more, open, so open. My tongue is everywhere, and you feel my teeth, biting, nibbling. Your face goes pained, a pained smile; your back arches, and your hands grip knuckle-white in the leather, just before the orgasm explodes—a silent fireball—and goes up the center of your body. A column of electrical voltage fires the warm, deep-red blossoms in your mind, and you are cumming, cumming so hard. You are motionless for a moment before your pussy shoots a long gush of juice, and you are bucking and grinding and riding the tongue and lips and teeth that are eating your orgasms out of you as they happen. You fall slowly and deliberately forward to touch your forehead and then to lay your head on my knees as your pussy expels another orgasm. Your body is racked with spasms. Your knees slide out to the insides of the armrests, lowering your face down as your cheek brushes my knees. Your hands are on my shins, and your gut muscles tighten in sudden spasms as you stutter whimpers and hang on with both hands. Your mind subconsciously struggles to remember another time when you orgasmed this hard, this many times, this completely.

Your breathing slows as you feel my focus shift up to your hood and clit. The warm, wide tip of my tongue slides over and around, searching expertly and surely. Your back arches down again, and your ass goes up slightly. A new part of your pussy is delivered to the tongue and teeth that are blowing your mind, the lips and licking and biting on the sensitive, hidden pleasure spots that you thought only you knew. Your head presses down on my knees as the hints and wisps of orgasms start to form again. Your eyes close, your mouth opens, your body knowing what to expect.

CHAPTER 2

Needed

A soft kiss on your lips, my hands on your waist; you feel one of my hands going to the front of your pants. You feel the clasp being unhooked.

"Oh no … we shouldn't."

You feel my hand cup over your pants, over your mound; you feel my hand pressing firmly and lifting you slightly. Your pussy reacts instantly, and you feel your clit beginning to throb. Your face goes slack, and you stop talking; your stomach goes fluttery, and your nipples harden. The man hand presses hard against your itchy, needy cunt, and you give, you give in. Your eyes soften, and your lower lip quivers slightly. The sweet pain of needing and getting on your face as you feel both of my hands on the front of your pants; your pants are opened and yanked down. The room air plays on your open crotch and panties in the momentary pause of you with your pants down before I lean on you and kiss your neck. You feel my hand, strong and warm, and knowingly move your panties aside. Three of my fingers, tight together, raft up and down on your wet slit.

My hand, firm and demanding, works your juicy cunt up and down as you are pressed back to the counter, not saying anything and not wanting to say anything. The pleasures are spreading and warming, filling your body. Your breasts feel full and taut and needy, and your nipples get so hard. You hope I look at them; you hope I touch them. Your knees go weak as your pussy balloons and throbs. Your hands touch me for a moment before they go back to the counter and grip the edge.

You feel your whole body shaking and mushy with the need to be fucked. My other hand comes up suddenly and calmly to your blouse, and you feel my hand press on your chest below your chin. As I grip your blouse, the fabric goes tight, causing a sudden hard tug and the tup, tup, tup of buttons coming off. Another move of my hand and your bra is yanked down, your breasts exposed, lewd and sexual, lifted up and uncomfortable by the bra shoved under and banded beneath them. Your mouth opens, and your face goes pleading and sad as your orgasm is welling up and owning you. You can't contribute, can't speak; sorry, so sorry. This orgasm is coming, it's coming hard.

I push you down to the floor suddenly. You land on your shins and go to your back with your pants yanked down and your shirt ripped open. The bra strap cuts into your swollen breasts; you don't feel anything but the cum knot throbbing and growing in your cunt. You glance up and stare at my pants, down to my hard cock, jutting out rude and mean, my hand fisting it, prepping it. It needs to feel fucking, and it wants your cunt. You dare to look up into my eyes, and you are terrified at the stranger you see there. As your pussy senses the nearness of hard animal cock, it opens even more.

I go to my knees, and you are still staring, your heart racing, your mouth moving with silent *no, no, please no.* Your elbows are out wide, and your hands are on your breasts. Your fingers are tight, squeezing your nipples. My hands are on your legs, and you are rolled over without any look from me, no grin, no sparkle, no game play. The fear heats you ice-vodka hot, and you moan, with the side of your face on the floor. Your hips are lifted up and back, familiar and unfamiliar; your ass cheeks are grabbed hard and spread without soft words or consideration, spread a little too far apart. Your asshole feels it, feels the stretch. This isn't your bedroom, and you have no say, no control. When the dry, iron finger violates your unprepared rosebud and spears deep into your ass, you cry out in pain but also in pleasure, a guttural, lunging growl from your gut. As you lower your shoulders, you press your ass back into the pain, and you are craven now, wanton and lewd and lusting on a primal level. The pain of two fingers opens your ass, sending you closer and closer to the orgasm you desperately need.

Then the fingers are gone, and the empty hole feels soreness. Your mind barely has time to register it before the real push, the real pressure. Any feeling in your asshole is lost in the brutality. It's all happening inside your ass, the queasy, fluttery feeling in your gut, and the cock filling your ass. A pulsing organ fills your ass, and your ass isn't yours anymore. You begin to shake; your perverted, filthy fantasies are in full-on mode, and your body is responding and giving in and going with it.

Your face is on the tiles, your hands flat, and your elbows up. Your body feels overfilled and rounded around the huge cock owning your lower body, the huge cock that has mercifully stopped advancing, bottomed out deep inside you. It's a telephone pole. You feel yourself sliding back with it as the cock is slowly drawn back. Your arms go straight and in front of you. You feel from a distance the apple of the head stretching your abused and numbed asshole open from the inside going out, and you start to cum. Your pussy spasms, your stomach tightens, and you begin to cum. You get the feeling there is a mountain of an orgasm starting inside you, and it's incredible. You just want to be held and played with and tended to. You cry out and cum and cum until you are spent.

Your breath stalls in your chest, and you are not thinking, barely being, suspended in the sudden ramming violence, the chaotic explosion of pain and pleasure. Your ass is physically yanked back hard by the sudden thrust of cock deep into your ass.

The side of your face slides in tiny movements on the tile, as your body takes the thudding slamming of my hips. Your ass is battered and surrendered and gloved loosely around the throbbing, erect cock mercilessly deep in your bowels, with heavy, cum-swollen balls and a primal self-absorbed desperate need to empty them at any cost.

Barely keeping yourself up, your mind is in a haze of sex and submission and pleasure. You feel my body pressing on yours, and you collapse flat on your stomach. The floor crushes your breasts painfully, and still the animal ass-fucking continues. Your pussy is pressed onto the cold tile by the thrusting cock in your ass, and you cum again. You hear my groaning behind you, and you feel your ass taking a final spearing thrust before I cry out. You feel the rapid tapping of male seed coating your bowels, continuing for long moments before you feel the spent cock leaving your ass and I fall beside you, breathing hard.

CHAPTER 3

Stall

Straightening up, you place the saddle blankets over the stall rails. The after-lunch sun beats down outside the wide-open doors of the barn, and you are busy. Your husband and kids are going to the movies for the afternoon two towns over, and you have the place to yourself; no interruptions. You run your hand for a moment over the flank of the horse standing patiently and contentedly in the stall and allow yourself a moment to breathe, just breathe. The sunlight is coming in angled through the open doors, and the dust is settling. You take in the smell of a clean barn and the saddles in their places, the leather oiled and tended to; you look around one more time and are thinking about heading in when you see the pickup truck coming down and the cloud of dust behind it.

You step out of the barn and stand waiting for the visitor to arrive. The truck gets to the gates, slows, and turns into the main yard, parking in the right place. You nod to yourself and begin to walk over. The driver's-side door opens at the same time, and you recognize the man getting out—Dan from that Blue Seal over in the next county. Their store is bigger than the feed store in town, and he's a nice guy; he knows a lot. You watch him coming toward you, and you start walking toward him. He covers the short distance between you with an easy, long stride in boots used to walking on dirt.

"Hi! I'm sorry to be coming by and bothering you like this, but we had a little bit of a problem with finding dry rot in the last shipment of hay we got in. Some of our customers reported the problem to us, and we've been covering their purchase with fresh hay replacements. Anyway, your name and farm were among those listed on the deliveries made from that shipment of bad hay, and I'm stopping by today to see if you had any problems."

"With the hay … no, no problems. We haven't had any problem so far."

"If you'd like, I'd be happy to take a look for you, free of charge. It's in our company's return policy. Also, I have to complete a visual inspection form for every farm on the list."

"Oh, of course. Right this way."

"Thank you. It shouldn't take long."

He's nodding and you're nodding, and it's all good, very routine and normal. The sun beats down on his Stetson hat and his crisp white-collared shirt and his jeans—the cowboy businessman, earnest and polite. His smile and those jeans and those boots, the buckle; your eyes follow up the buttons of his shirt, over that flat stomach to the tanned neck, and then your eyes meet his. It's only a moment, a few seconds, one quick glance, and he is staring into your eyes with a calm, piercing strength that holds you with a hard glint and a real understanding. Your eyes narrow, and you breathe out and touch the tip of your tongue to the roof of your mouth, getting a sudden fluttery feeling in your stomach and a tingly twinge way back in your pussy. You push your jaw out and breathe out and look away, pointing to the barn and listening for his boot steps in the dirt before you glance up at the back of his shirt and fall in behind him.

"Right this way. We keep our hay up in this loft."

He enters the barn ahead of you and is looking up, walking slowly as he studies the bales. You stand there politely, looking up at the bales too but also looking at the clipboard being held by those hands and his pen moving on the paper. He's a nice guy; he knew the model of the pump and the part that went bad that time and the other time coming back now. You were at his Blue Seal store, looking at the seed selection, and he happened by and you started talking about hybrid vs. that new genetic seed. He said the hybrid was working well on ten acres he set aside on his own farm, and you said you'd stay with the hybrid then too. He smiled that same warm smile, and his eyes did that same calm, knowing thing, and yeah, you remember him better now.

With everyone gone and no distractions, there is nothing pressing, and you allow a little bit of daydreaming as you watch. His shoulders move under that shirt, those muscled legs when he moves … and yeah, that tight ass. Definitely tight.

"Well, I don't see any dry rot problem. You look good." He is facing you and tucking his pen into the top of the clipboard, calm and sure of himself. It's all good and normal and businesslike. You watch him lowering the clipboard down to his side, and he is still facing you. You feel suddenly awkward, outwardly calm but suddenly needy—no no, easy, girl. The tingle goes to a low thrum down there, and you feel your nipples tingling. It's best this visit ends right now.

"Like I said, you look good, except that you have your bales going the wrong way. Yours are sideways, and they need to go lengthways. More efficient."

"Excuse me?"

"You heard me. Your bale placement sucks."

"What? Who the hell—"

"Damned amateurs."

"The hell are you talking to—?"

"Look. Right there. Bales lying sideways. Wasted room. And there. Same thing."

You are looking into those eyes, and they are piercing right through you. The fluttery feeling is rising in your stomach, and the shaky feeling is all over. You look away with effort and turn away, taking a step toward the loft, pretending to look up, your stomach tightening. He should leave; he should just leave now, with his hat and shoulders and those eyes.

"See 'em?"

He is behind you now, close behind you. It's all good; it's all still good—the heat of the barn and the hay and his cologne. You are nodding, looking up, not seeing but nodding, and he should just go. Really for the best, just go—

"If I saw my kids stacking like that, they'd all get a spanking ... every one of 'em."

"Just for ... uh ... stacking hay the wrong way? Doesn't seem very—"

"Spanking works. Get them over your knee and redden their butts for them and it's over ... lesson learned."

"That's it ... lesson learned."

"Right, pants down and a flat hand."

This is crazy. You barely know this guy, and even If you did, you are married. He's only here to check the hay, and you both know it. Of course, yes, but here we are in another long moment, aren't we? You swallow and try to think and get yourself back on track, but your pulse is racing, and you are seeing his hand and his lap in your mind and your ass up on his lap. *Oh fuck, stop this, stop this right now.*

You breathe out a stuttering breath, and you are looking up at the rafters. Your right foot is back and resting nervously on the toe of your boot, and your hand goes lightly to the stable wood as you pretend to look.

"Pants down."

You hear his words, low and measured and calm, and you freeze up, staring down now at the wood and your hand. You didn't hear that, not the way it sounded; he's still talking about his kids—

"Turn around. Look at me."

Your hand is gripping hard on the wood now, and you want to move, to turn around and face him but, you can't, not for a hundred reasons. Your stomach is tight, and below that, your pussy is a throbbing, wet mess. Your legs feel like numb stone as your hand goes to the saddle blanket, just to touch it.

"Turn around and come here. If I have to come over there, you aren't going to like it."

His words are warm and firm and very clear; they go straight to the hidden, secret part of your mind. You almost bend over from the sudden, thick twinge in your gut. You stroke the blanket with your hand, and for a moment, it's this morning again, and you are laying out the blankets, all alone with your thoughts. You breathe out and bite your lip and force yourself to turn around. Your hand leaves the blanket, and you are standing, facing him. The doors of the barn are still open, and the yard is outside in the sunshine, and you could just walk, just walk right on by him, and this would be over. Never happened, nothing ever happened; out those doors and get some air, and he would come out and apologize politely and awkwardly and drive off in his truck.

You start walking. You are staring out the doors when you stop, standing in front of him. He is sitting in the old wooden chair, the straight-back, no-arms wooden chair that was part of the barn forever. Now you glance up from your looking down enough to see the lap and the boots, before you look down again.

"That's it ... good girl." His voice is warm and soothing.

"Lower your jeans, sweet one."

Staring down, straight down, your hands come up to the front of your jeans by themselves, and you watch your fingers finding the stud. You watch your fingers undo the stud and the slight opening of your jeans. You watch your right hand go to the top of the zipper and your fingers find the tab and pull the tab, easing down, down, to the bottom. Your jeans open wide, your panties showing in the V; your hands go to the sides, and your thumbs hook the belt loops.

Down to your hips and then down past your hips. His hand comes into your view, and you put your hand out, taking hold, not looking up as you are guided to the side of his lap. The hand goes gently to your shoulder as you bend your knees and lower yourself. His hand goes wide and firm, barely touching electric on the panties covering your ass cheek, and you are going over. You straighten your arms, and your hands touch on the straw on the floor as you feel your stomach settling on his lap. It's real now, very real; the straw under your hands and the firm warmth of the lap under your stomach. Your legs are half bent, and your boots toes down, barely down and barely thinking, before you feel a hand lay itself on the small of your back and fingers easing under the thin band of your panties. He's pulling up and pulling back, and you feel the warm air of the room on your ass cheeks, the firm yank taking your panties down, and then the light touches on your calves. You feel your panties down around your ankles, the air on your cheeks.

Both of your legs are bent at the knee, and your hands are flat in front of you, you feel his hand lay soft on your ass cheek as you move slightly on his lap. He hears your whispered "Oh, God" as his hand begins to glide around in slow circles on your bare skin. He hears your hiss and whoosh of breath and sees you moving your arms out wider, your hands pressing flat again and your boots digging in. He looks down at your ass and his hand moving gently over the bare skin. His cock swells in his jeans as he traces up and over and down the smooth skin of the cheek and back up again. His hand goes over the crack and lands gently on the other cheek, going to the top near your hip and grazing up, over and down, down to the small of your ass cheek and back up to the top.

You lift your head and lower it again as his hand goes smoothly down to the small of your ass cheeks and stays there. His fingertips touch and brush lightly on your sensitive labia. Your legs go to a quarterback crouch as his fingers rub gently on the insides of your thighs, just below your pussy, before he straightens his middle finger down and runs the rounded tip smooth and quick up your wet slit and your ass crack. You raise your head and hold yourself tight as he brings his middle finger back down and runs up your slit and this time over your puckering asshole. Your head goes down low to the floor, as your ass goes up and your cheeks spread. You hold back whimpers as he brings his thick middle finger down and places the tip of his hard cock at your dripping pussy hole, moving the tip in tiny circles in your juices before sliding the glistening tip roughly, plowing up your slit and over your throbbing asshole. He lets the tip of his middle finger catch in the middle of the wrinkled pucker and slide out. You cry out, squirming, breathing deep, your pussy and ass on fire.

You breathe in short gasps, and the back of your throat feels tight. His hand is flat and firm, gliding over your ass cheeks now. Your pussy is dripping, muscular, and greedy; your gut thrumming, your throbbing asshole itching for a hard cock, and you are committed. You can't go back; you won't go back. You have to cum, you have to cum. Please, sir.

Whap! ... Whap whap!

The noise fills the room, sharp and loud, and you hear the sound and feel the sudden heat at the same time, lifting and straightening your back. Your cunt presses itself onto the hardness of his lap, and you go back down, groaning loudly.

Whap! ... Whap!

Two more on your ass with the sound, the impact of his hand, and your ass warming now. Your feet kick back, and you try to catch your breath.

Whap! ... Whap! Whap!

You take the hand harder on your ass now, and the pain rises up, a warm blanket to your mind. Your arms are straight; your hands are moving by themselves in the straw. You are watching them and trying to process the orgasm fisting up, barreling up huge in your cunt. Ohh, God.

Whap whap whap whap whap!

"Ohhhhhh Godddddd!"

His hand lands rapidly and hard on your deeply reddened ass before sliding down to your swollen cunt. You feel the three fingers enter, tight and deep, and your breath catches in your throat. You are going to cum; you are going to cum. The fingers bunch roughly, fucking your juicy, hungry cunt. You groan again as you feel it in your ass crack, on your asshole, the thick stump and sudden burn of a dry thumb pressing itself lewdly into your rosebud. Your mouth opens in a silent scream. In the same moment, you feel yourself pushed, and you are off his lap and onto the floor, the dirt floor of the barn, jeans down and panties down, ass and pussy exposed for everyone to see.

But ohhh God, you have to cum, please, you have to cum now. You go to your hands and knees, and you feel his presence suddenly by your side, just as suddenly a warm weight on your back. His hand reaches under, and it's a strap, oh God, a pony strap. You have a pony saddle on your back, and the holding strap is pulled tight against your stomach. You turn yourself away and try to crawl, but his hands are on your hips, and you are halted, stopped. You are trying to process the saddle on your back. You arch your back down and lift your head and scream, whimper into the rafters. The sudden spearing of thick cock goes directly through and up to your mouth, and you are whimper-screaming. The saddle is on your back, and your cunt is suffering a direct and ruthless cocking. You go down to your elbows, and the thick oak pole in your cunt goes into a deep stroke that shreds any thought as your gut tightens, huge with an orgasm that explodes from everywhere in your body at once. You are cumming, screaming and gripping at the dirt and cumming.

The second, third, fourth—you lose count of the orgasms blooming up and exploding on top of each other. You get to your forearms, your thighs wet with pussy juice and your whimpering grunts pushed in short yelps from your throat by the cock thrusting in your cunt. You are about to lower your head again when the thrusting stops abruptly. A shiver wracks your body as you feel the thick shaft of penis slid roughly back and gone and your pussy left gaping in the barn air. Shaking, feeling woozy and dazed, you go to your hands on shaky arms, breathing hard from your fucking and thinking about getting up.

Thwack!

You hear the whistling, high-pitched whisper, and your mind recognizes it, unable to process further before the thin blade of the riding crop connects and bites into your ass with a searing white-hot pain that widens your eyes. You scream out, surprised and genuinely in pain and confused.

Thwack!

"Pony girl, you need to move now."

You swallow hard and scream out and try to turn your head to reply, to ask why, to beg.

The handle of the crop pokes at your dripping cunt, as you squeal in surprise and excitement. You are so turned on, you can barely think. The handle's leather is smooth, and his cock is hard, poking at your cunt and swollen labia. You have no choice; you want to please, just to please. You put your arm forward and then the other arm and then your back knee brought forward. You are crawling, freshly fucked and saddled, crawling on the dirty floor of your own barn, and you are on fire.

Thwack!

You stop crawling, your body tensed as the new line across your ass goes red fire into a cold heat, painful searing.

Thwack! Thwack! Thwack!

Teeth gritted, sweating, your knees bind in your lowered jeans, and you are trying your best to crawl, but it's difficult. Your jeans are down, and your humiliation and your pussy thrum, bloating up with orgasms.

The butt of the crop handle is jabbing into your cunt, and you feel fresh humiliation as you almost push back on it before catching yourself and obediently crawling forward. The handle sinks in deeper and lifts your backside suddenly.

His soft firm voice is encouraging and firm, and speaking to you like you are a horse. Your pussy twinges so badly, you whimper softly. Your mind races as your deepest fantasies are coming out in the open, easily and totally beyond your control.

CHAPTER 4

Garden Party

It is the first party of the summer, and you are so ready for it. The day is sunny and hot, the evening cooling slightly, with an occasional whisper of a warm breeze. You decide to wear your white blouse, with no bra, your tightest jeans, and sandals. You touch your hair last minute as you looked in the hall mirror and, yeah, all good. You head out the door feeling good, feeling ready, ready to party, and you crank the classic rock on the drive over to the party.

Arriving fashionably late to a decent crowd, you are served a glass of chilled white wine and mingle easily with your friends. You glance around from time to time and notice me noticing you. We smile small smiles at each other and continue to mingle, getting closer as the evening wears on. You are noticing my shoulders, my easy smile, the thick groomed hair, the cute ass, and I've checked out your chest under that sexy blouse, the sparkle in your eyes when you laugh, your long legs, down to your sandals. It's all good; the conversations have lasted for a while, and you glance around and wonder if maybe I left. That would suck, really.

"Hi."

"Hi."

"Nice to meet you. Forgive me, but I couldn't help but notice how much you want to see the backyard."

You laugh. *He's just being funny.* And with the wine and the party and your mood, you decide to play along, looking at me skeptically with a wary, warm smile. "As a matter of fact, I do."

"It was obvious. I just didn't want to see you embarrass yourself."

"Embarrass myself?" You play along. I'm clearly joking, and you can see that, and there is something else. The twinkle in my eyes. You feel a tingle on your back before I lift my hand to yours, and we walk casually through the party guests to the back sliding doors. I slide the glass open, and you step out ahead of me out into the warm evening air.

We sit outside on the back patio, sharing a bottle of wine. The time flies by as we talk and laugh, hardly noticing the other guests leaving, hardly noticing the first bottle of wine long gone and now most of the second bottle—and really not caring about either fact. We are liking that we like each other.

We sit in the reclining lawn chairs, the candle flickering on the small table between us as we look up at the stars, the quiet and the intimacy growing. We hear a polite knock on the glass and then the sliding door opening just a crack.

"Guys, it's been a great party. You are welcome to stay as long as you like. We're going to turn in now. Thanks again for coming!"

We both stand up politely. "Sure, John," I answer. "Thanks for having us over."

"Sure thing. Good night."

The door eases closed. You are still looking at the glass doors.

"But I haven't cum yet."

Your buzz strong, you are mortified to hear those words slip quietly out of your mouth, in the same moment equally surprised to feel my hands lightly on your hips.

"Hey!"

The hands turn you by your hips, and you are in my arms, the kiss slow and sensual, strange and familiar and sexy and warm.

"I'm having a great time with you. It's been a wonderful evening."

You are looking into my eyes, and you smile. You had—are having—a wonderful time too. The moment of potential embarrassment has passed away and gone, and you put your arms around my waist and smile into my eyes. "Yes, me too. Thank you."

I smile back. "It's getting pretty late. We should do this again sometime."

"Yes, we should, definitely," you agree.

"I'll give you a call, and maybe we could go do something."

"I'd like that."

"Okay, then," I reply, "well, we really should be going, I guess. Oh, wait! You said you hadn't cum yet."

You look at me, mortified for a long moment, not sure what you are seeing in my eyes; warmth, mostly, sexy warmth and a glint of something else. You smile and try to look as calm as the man holding you, but your patient pussy twinges hard, and you swallow, quick and hard, before replying. "You heard that."

"Yes."

"It slipped out."

"I know."

It's only a moment, really, but we are looking into each other's eyes, and so many things are being said and understood and agreed to. Those sparkling, knowing eyes aren't looking away; they are looking right into you, and your stomach is fluttering, and your nipples feel hard as hell, and your pussy is a thrumming, tight, quivering, juicy mess.

"We—I—I should go."

You bring your arms down and step away, stand there a moment and look down and around like you are looking for your purse. But you didn't bring one, silly, horny girl. You need to just be going already. I turn and go to the edge of the patio. I reach down and pick up something. In the dim light, it's hard to see as I turn around calmly.

I appear with the hose nozzle in my hand; you know what it is now, and you also see the water dripping from it. You stare at the nozzle in my hand and the end pointing at you.

"We need to be quiet about this," I say.

Suddenly my hand is squeezing, and the hose jumps a little. A stream of water is coming out of the hose, and you are hit. You are wet; your blouse is wet, see-through now. The water runs down on your jeans and back up on your breasts, hitting your nipples. Your hand goes out to the back of the chair for support, and you are looking at me, then at the patio stones, and then back at me, barely seeing me, thanking me as you feel the shudder and the sudden coming together deep inside your pussy. Your knees bend as the orgasm balls up and emerges and explodes deep inside you. The water hits you in short bursts on your stomach and directly on your tits as you go to your knees, cumming hard again.

Your knees slide outward in the puddling water around you. You bring your palms up at the solid stream of water that is playing across your breasts, snapping stings on your hard nipples and mauling on your breasts through the wet, thin fabric. Your hand slides off the edge of the chair, and you cum again, hard, not believing this is happening and not caring. You can't keep up as the orgasms come one after another. You bring your hands to your stomach as the spasms explode large in your cunt. You fall forward gently and to your side, groaning quietly through gritted teeth, when you just want to scream out. Your arm is out, and you lay your head on it and breathe hard and sob. "Oh my God, that was …"

You feel hands at your hips and fingers on the band of your jeans, and your jeans are unbuttoned. You look up and back through your blurred vision and see that it's me. Your jeans are unzipped, and I am tugging them down like we've done this a hundred times before. It doesn't matter anyway; you are too far gone. This is too incredible; your jeans are tugged off, and your naked legs are on the patio stone, and there's the hands again and your panties, tugged down and off. You move your legs up; your ass is lifting. You are trying to get to your hands and knees at least. *What if anyone is awake in the house? Oh my God, we should stop. We should.*

The hard stream of water goes directly into your crotch, a short burst of water that three-fingers your pussy and gooses your puckering asshole. You let out a gasp and know you have to move on some level. You manage to move one knee, and you begin to crawl. The water is dripping from you, and you are wet, so very wet. Your head is down, and there is the dark on the edge of the patio, and you should go toward there.

A second sluicing burst of water reaches your spasming cunt and stays until you cum with an orgasm sudden and intense. The water stops, and you manage to go up on one knee to turn to say something. What you don't know is that I have come around to face you, and you see the nozzle and then the short bursts of water, the tight streams of water on your right breast and left breast and back again. Short, stinging needle bursts of bulls-eye water on your rock-hard nipples. Your face goes taut as you tighten into another orgasm.

At a house you've never been to before, you are on your hands and knees, half-naked, soaked, with a man you just met standing calmly a few feet away with a hose—and it's all good, so fucking good. You bite your lip as you feel your submission. You begin to crawl again toward the edge of the patio, to the grass, to get away, knowing you don't stand a chance.

The stream hits your ass cheeks first, and the force stings. You get the last two feet to the cool grass before the cock-hard stream hits your cunt and your arms give out. You are face down on the grass with your ass up as the water hits your cheeks again, before the stream homes in and stays on your cunt. You grip blindly and hard on the grass, and you cum again, beyond embarrassed and humiliated. I know what you like and what you are. You are cumming hard, and the water finger moves slightly and pushes hard on your asshole, a million tongues and fingers on your sensitive asshole, and you can hardly breathe.

Your face and hands are down in the wet grass. The warm water is blunt and hard on your tight hole. You push back against the stream, and the stream stretches on your asshole. The tremors of pleasure starburst through your body. The stream line is passing rapidly back and forth over your asshole, and you let out a throaty cry and fall to your side, rolling helplessly onto your back, gasping and blinking away the water. The breeze feels warm over your wet blouse and legs, and you are staring up into the night at nothing. Your knees are up; the water starts again, hits your shins before your legs fall open from surprise and fatigue, and the water is centered suddenly on your mound, rudely up and down on your slit and clit. Your knees go diagonally apart, your arms out and flat on the lawn, and you are gripping at the grass, taking it, lying motionless and open as the hose shoots water violently and generously on your open cunt. The unstoppable overstimulation sends you into another mind-blanking orgasm.

You open your eyes, breathing hard, blinking away the water in your eyes. You take a deep breath to calm yourself, and you try to think. Startled from your thoughts by my hands at your side, you turn your head toward me as I slide my hands underneath and lift you easily, standing up and cradling you in my arms as I walk us back to the patio. You have snuggled your face into my neck, and it just feels right, so comfortable. My clothes are warm and reassuring on your wet skin as we walk. We get to the patio, and I lay you down in the recliner, warm and comfortable with several thick beach towels that have been placed on it. You lie back on the back rest, and I carefully lay a large towel over you. I then go into the house and return a few minutes later with two glasses of wine. I hand you a glass and sit down in the other recliner. We both take a sip and look at each other, the patio torches flickering.

CHAPTER 5

Tea

You smile to yourself before you turn slowly in your chair to look at me on the floor, naked, a few feet away. My shins are flat on the carpet, my thigh muscles defined. I am leaned back; you used the white silk rope this time. My elbows and forearms are on the carpet, my forearms bound to my calves with neat rows of the rope. You take it all in before you bring your eyes to my cock. Smiling to yourself, almost grinning, you shake your head gently as you see the size of my hard-on jutting straight and hard and angling back with me. The head is like a tiny helmet perched on top of the swollen shaft. You relish the veins and the girth and the pinkish skin as your eyes travel down, almost giggling again as you see my balls, hard little marbles in that tight sack. The excitement must be pretty great, poor dear, and you are only grading papers. Tsk tsk. Your eyes leave my groin and go back up, lingering over my defined stomach muscles before reaching my face. Your heart goes out to me, and your pussy is tingling as you see the look of concentration, the set jaw, my eyes down—as they should be.

You get up from your chair and stretch, glancing over your rope work and your bound toy below you before you head to the kitchen for a cup of tea.

Your tea-warmed mouth is on the sensitive head of my cock. I can feel the tip of your soft, pretty tongue harvesting the precum from the slit, with your calm and friendly way and your soft voice. You reach under and cradle my balls in your tender grip. You are reading my mind now, ordering me not to cum as my eyes mist. It takes all of my effort not to, defines my muscles further. My jaw goes tighter, and I just barely keep down the cum boiling in my balls. Your firm voice encourages, "This is not the time, not the time." I'm your alpha man toy, bound for your pleasure, your visual and tactile fun while you grade papers. You sit by my side, cross-legged, sipping your tea casually. My cock is a hard bone, genuinely aching for relief, harder than I have ever felt it. My balls feel ready to burst, sensitive as they thrum quietly in your hand, unstroked, unattended to, but so very happy for your palm.

I won't look up; I know my place. I won't look up, because I know the intense need for you is in my eyes, the need to feel pain for you, a yearning ache inside me. I'm picturing you with your cane or whip, standing in our finished basement, my back and ass welted and striped. My breath catches in my throat, and I almost gag with need, seeing you with a strap-on and going deep red before pushing the thought frantically from my mind. I concentrate on my thighs, staring at my thighs, your sweet voice helping me to hang on.

My eyes are wide, and I stare at you as you lift your cup of tea to my lips. I take a grateful sip, the liquid momentarily soothing my parched mouth. A gallon wouldn't be enough. You have me on the edge of cumming, and you keep every muscle tight in my body, every nerve tingling and bright. My heart is racing, and my hard-on bobbing by itself from the tension and your attentions. I remind myself that it is there for your pleasure, your amusement—and we continue, me naked and bound, rock-hard and frustrated; you, calm and sophisticated, womanly and academic, warm and friendly but firm, very firm. This is the most intense experience I have ever had, and I don't want it to end. Looking down at my cum-loaded cock, I thank God I don't have to speak, afraid my masculine voice will come out weepy and needy.

With a quick, harsh breath, my knees bend, my leg muscles define, and you feel me lifting my hips. That quivery, trembling feeling goes through you as you place your hand on my hips and press down gently, reminded again of the muscularity, of the animal beneath your hand. You look up at my closed eyes and grimacing mouth, and you know how much pleasure you are giving me, the effect you have on me. The other parts of your mind are working now, those other parts and those thoughts as you touch your lips gently on the helmet head of the gorgeous cock and feel my hips buck helplessly with real need. You press down again with your hand and exercise the needed control, looking up into my eyes as you think about training. You take your mouth away and hear my fevered sigh of disappointment, so you lay your hand, cool and soft, on the hot flesh of my hyper-excited cock, smiling your smile as you come up and sit close to my head, bringing your mouth close to my ear, whispering gently. "Maybe my stud boy needs a little more."

You move your hand and fingers loosely up and down the pulsing shaft. "I was thinking about a ride in the garden, getting the saddle on you and cinching it tight and going for a nice ride. See how my roses are doing."

To your delight, you see my jaw clench. You bring your hand up around the head of my cock and touch your fingertip in the cleft of the slit and feel the seepage, the precum. Your own pulse races, your mind filling with your favorite images of dominance, and your pussy a thick, wet mess.

"You know how much I enjoy riding you."

Changed into your riding clothes and carrying the black nylon bag containing the toys you will need, you get to the sliding glass doors and pause for a moment, looking out past the deck to the green grass of our secluded backyard. Looking at the magnificent view of your man, muscular and naked and on all fours, waiting patiently for his mistress, you feel the hint in your gut, and you breathe out, running the tip of your tongue quickly over your lips as you think of the orgasm—the *orgasms*—you are going to have later. Standing there in your riding outfit with your bag full of toys, you feel feminine and athletic and sexual. You stare out at your stud, waiting for you, and you feel loving and tender and dominant. The scent of me lingers around you, and you put your hand on the handle and begin to slide open the door. Feeling fit and ready to fuck, you step out into the sunshine and walk across the deck, down the stairs to the yard. Your nipples are hard and your breasts full, your pussy and ass are tight and tingling. The grass brushes the bottoms of your boots as you stroll, confident and focused, toward me.

With a second bite on that taut flesh, the skin between your teeth, the taste, the scent of your animal breathed in deep and raising your own level of sexual lust to new heights. You open your mouth and release the skin, and you glide your hand over the dark-red welts. Your face remains calm and serious and intense with lust as you ease out your tongue and lick. Such a fine beast, such a fuck stud, muscular and obedient, so dedicated to you.

Reluctantly you move your mouth away from the hard, rounded cheek and move your eyes to the space between the cheeks. You place your hands as a good trainer would and spread the cheeks, parting the two globes to expose the tight ring of puckered muscle. You breathe out again, and with calm eyes you bring your hand up, extending your middle finger and touching the ball tip to the center, pressing very gently, feeling the snug kiss of the sphincter and the firm resistance of a healthy male anus. You lift and stroke your finger gently on it for a moment, caressing strokes on the sensitive skin that are an owner's treat for her well-behaved steed, sugar-cube rewards of intimate touches straight from the hand of a mistress to her pet.

You pick up the butt plug and look at it for a moment, orientating the balled end of the handle toward my ass. You bring it up and touch the end gently to my crack, feeling the dry hardness of the plastic drag on the skin as it sits on the crack, wedged slightly, suspended above and too big to go down to the hole. Then you pick up the lube, get the tip close, and squeeze a few drops, watching them land in the center and the wrinkled sides. It's not as much as you'd like to put there but better than the nothing you know I would have preferred. You move the butt plug forward and back, watching it pivot on the ball snugged in the crack. You might have gone with a smaller size, but there was insistence in my red face and my adamant way as we stood together in front of the display that day. Your alpha male, your executive, your manly man was trying to keep his voice low. His face was beet red and very cute as he moved your wandering hand repeatedly to the horse-cock end of the display, as he quietly and earnestly argued his case for you to use the biggest plug they had.

You sigh and nod to yourself at the memory, your pussy humming as you press the ball down, using your arm muscles to get the ball close enough to touch on the gel. The size of the ball easily outclasses the tiny, glistening pucker below it, and you thank me silently for allowing you to use any lube at all, appreciating again my need to gift you with my pain. You feel your pussy tingle—such a good slave. You've eased up, but now you press hard again, the veterinarian push. You feel the rounded, blunt end of the butt plug make contact with the sphincter, and you push again with your full weight, feeling the plug penetrate and pop in. One more quick push to seat the base. You pause to check, pleased to see there is no damage. The sphincter stays thin and tight around the hard plastic of the plug. You grab the tail of the plug and give a careful tug; the plug remains deep and tight, and you are satisfied.

I feel tears on my face and then your cool hands and your sweet, sweet kiss. Time stops, pleasure becomes all thought as you straddle yourself over my thick, pulsing cock and lower yourself slowly down. Your tightness feels wet like soothing rain. Seeing your teary eyes and the meaningful look you are giving me, I have no words as you sheath my cock safely inside you.

Chapter 6

Stopping By

"Hi … just thought I'd stop by real quick."

"Hey! Hi! Sure, come on in."

Your pussy twinged as soon as you saw my head through the back door. Coming to your house was an unexpected surprise. As you came through the kitchen, you remembered that you did mention how empty the neighborhood was this time of day or something like that. Your pulse quickens, and your nipples harden.

Your hand opens the screen door, and you see me, see the look in my eyes. I am in. You let out a breathy *unnnh!* as you are slammed to the wall, lips hard on yours, and your T-shirt being pulled up over your head. Looking down, you see your shirt hit the floor before the sudden scalp burn. Your head is lifted up hard by your hair; my mouth is slobbery and animalistic on your neck. You feel your jeans being tugged at and opened and ripped down, hard hands on your thighs, and your panties going down. Your knees bend, and your back slides on the wall as you watch my arm moving back and my hand coming forward with a black tie-down from the back of my pickup. I rope the wide nylon band around your tit and pull it painfully tight, the clicking of the mechanical ratchet tightening the band until it locks. I reach behind and bring up another tie-down, wrapping it around the base of your other tit and yanking it tight in the same way. The clicking and the snap locks the ratchet. Both of your breasts are roped tight and locked in less than a minute, and you are hardly moving.

Your eyes are closed and you're breathing hard against the wall. Two rough fingers suddenly force knuckles deep into your cunt, and you almost cum. Your pussy grips the fingers fucking their way in and out. Your knees give, and you sink down, whispering, whimpering, protesting the third finger joining the fuck. Your eyes close tightly, and you grimace with pain, pleasure, and need as you are squatting and the fourth finger is added. You shudder. *Yes-yes-yes-ohh-fuck,* and wince as the pussy-slick fingers form a fist and the fist corkscrews slowly and muscled up into your cunt and you cum, hard, squatting helplessly with your full weight down on the fist, deep, deep in your spasming pussy. Your hands come down blindly and find the biceps, gliding fingertip kisses as your cunt takes the strong-arm fist fuck and you cry out, held in place, cumming again as your neck is kissed and bitten.

You're breathing hard, still jerking and spasming on the fist as you feel it pulled slowly and unapologetically from your abused and stretched cunt. Your knees and body are weak as you slide down to the floor, your ass barely on the tile before the first hit of cock on the side of your face. The soft, hard bone slaps on the hollow of your cheek and back again; the hard rap and then a rapid back-and-forth that pummels your face before you feel my hand grip hard in your hair and the sudden probing shoves of cock head on your lips. You reflex gag on my cock head as it wedges itself to the back of your throat. Hard, muscled, sweaty thighs press on the sides of your head, and the silent pop of sudden pain from my cock in the back of your mouth, forcing down into your throat. The back-and-forths of a man's body, tooling his cock in your throat before he fucks it without concern, and you feel your pussy squirt. Your hands go down to your thighs, going limp and not reaching your pussy as the cock gets itself balls-deep and you feel both legs moving it up and down in the tightness of your unready throat.

My hands grip painfully on your head as you grunt. The stretching pain and heat continue in your throat as your thoughts go fragmented and spacey. The upstroke and pause and sudden ejaculate pump splatters warm and thick, filling your mouth. You feel the pulse of the penis and the hairy, weighted balls on your chin, until the pumping slows and stops and the ridged cock head passes out from your dragging lips, your mouth completely filled with cum.

CHAPTER 7

Fresh Grass

I pull you to me and kiss you hard; my tongue finds yours, taming it and sending a quivering tremor through your mind. Your body melts in just the way that blends you to me, melds you close and soft and intimate to me, to my arms and chest. You look down demurely, knowing you are the one making my cock rock hard; you are the one bringing out my dark side, all for your pleasure. The hard chest and muscled arms, the cock you've sucked—your place of worship and your playground and your safe haven. You glance up into the eyes that absolutely adore you, and you also know that those eyes have watched you, worshipped you, admired the beauty of you and the beauty of your body without pause—drinking you in as a man quietly respectful and possessed by you.

Your mouth is stuffed with the hard cock of your master; your hands grip and caress on my hard ass cheeks as you suck. Your shredded, cut-off clothes are left where they fell, all over the backyard. Now your back burns with a crisscrossing of deep-red whip marks, the aftermath of one of our little games. Your breasts are swollen and painful from the face-down ass-fuck on the picnic table and the forced trampoline show directly afterward.

Your knees, thankfully, are in the softness of the fresh-cut grass. Your hair is matted and wild, and your mouth is a swollen mess as you bob and suck. My hands press hard on the sides of your head, as you feel the sudden, excruciating burn of cock forcing deep into your throat. The penetration comes as a single heaving thrust that takes your air away, and you buck comically, your legs sliding on the dewy grass and your arms waving slowly in the darkness as we play cock-fuck your throat. I groan with the effort and don't stop until my hairy balls are resting comfortably on your chin. I'm enjoying the desperate, spasming massage of your straining throat muscles and your wide-open, panicky, calm eyes for a little longer than I should before I pull out, slow and dawdling. The head of my cock squeegees tightly on the sides of your throat; the pop is audible and embarrassing as the head comes up and clears your throat.

I look down into your eyes; both of us are breathing hard, grinning, as my eyes adore you. I lift you to your feet and kiss you full and gently on your beautiful, sweet lips.

Still kissing your lips, I pull back a little, pausing. My hands go to the front of your jeans and blindly find the stud, undoing it and tugging down the zipper as you look into my eyes with that demure, womanly look of yours that I love so much. I feel my cock going rock hard and throbbing as I yank your jeans down to your hips and then down to your thighs. I pull your panties down as I go to my knees, pulling your legs apart at your thighs and getting my hungry mouth on your delicious, ready pussy—whole mouth on mound, sucking hard and slurping at your moistness and your juices. I lap and bite on your flesh as you moan out loud and lie back on the grass, your knees up and your jeans down, my face at your crotch, eating your pussy hard for my pleasure.

Your hands touch my hair as you squirt a little and grip my tongue, easing in. I pull back and lap openly at your pussy. I reach up and clamp my hands on your hips and roll you over with a strength and suddenness, as you feel your ass cheeks spread and the sudden wetness of my warm tongue licking at your sweaty asshole. You hear my moaning, and it turns you on that I would get that pleasure from you. You say nothing as you ease your ass back, groaning to yourself with embarrassed pleasure at my tongue and mouth on your asshole. You feel me move behind you and then the baseball-like head of my cock plowing up and down your wet slit, the fist in your hair, and the hard tug and the tingling burn on your scalp as your head goes back. You choke, cough, and then scream out, low and guttural, as I squat and ram my cock balls-deep into your cunt with a lewd thrust that cool-burns your cunt walls before they ignite in a flaming heat. You're stoked without mercy by the all-out fuck that crushes your tits hard in the grass, your hair pulled taut in my gripping hand, my cock ramming your cunt as I take my pony girl for a hard ride.

My arm curls, and I have your hair gripped in my hand. I tug hard, demanding more. You arch your back down obediently and tilt your ass up, spreading your cheeks to display your puckering pink asshole. On your knees now, you move your knees slightly apart to offer your hanging fruit, the swollen labia and juicy slit of your sexy cunt. My cock pulses to steel-hard, smooth oak, and I acknowledge your efforts with an angled, muscled pounding that gets my cock unnaturally deep. Your heartfelt groans cut off as your cunt takes the full length of my cock and some ball sack with each spearing stroke. Your welcoming pussy surrenders and goes numb as your shoulders are slammed painfully down into the grass. Your hands go flat, pressing, trying to counter the punishing fuck.

Your head is tilted back, your hair taut and tugged hard again before your face goes down and your lips smear a kiss on the grass. The rapid, brutal fucking goes to measured, intentional, long strokes that shatter and ignite your guts. The spark ball forms and glows white; the dull, red, pounding heat sparkles in your mind, and you gush, slamming your cunt back and feeling cock in your stomach and lungs as your orgasm hits hard, punching your brain, blanking your mind, your hands sliding and your face in grass. The fuck beast leans over your upturned ass, joyriding southern style Saturday night on your fucked-senseless pussy. Your drooling mouth emits soundless moans, as your orgasms persist, continuous and ecstatic beneath the relentless fucking. A moment of reprieve, and then the barely felt gut shudder comes as you sense the cock sudden and deep in your ass, the humiliation pressing the buttons behind your closed eyes. You cum again, the squelching cock reaming your craving asshole, and you cry out, subjugated, enslaved, and completely pleasured.

Your pussy is dripping juices and spasming between your legs. My hands are tight on your hips, and the hard pushes of my cock impaling your ass are too random to defend against. Your eyes are tearing, and your pussy is rag-pile sloppy with orgasms about to explode. You are down on your forearms, and your ass is straight up. The sudden weighted press of my chest on your back combines with the thud of my hips on your ass cheeks as your gut registers the ramming home of thick cock.

Hard on your breast, hard metal on your breast and nipple. Your face is close; you look down to see the chrome of the clamp, and the nausea of an intense orgasm needing to happen overtakes you. You see but barely feel, see and stare as your tit is scooped up in a rough hand and crushed. Your hard nipple is forced straight up, and the other hand stuffs the metal clamp down on your nipple. The tip of your nipple emerges dark and painfully red in the chrome as the screw is turned and turned. Your nipple goes pencil-point tiny; your eyes fill with sympathy tears as the pain explodes in your mind, starshine bright and exhilarating and freeing. You continue to stare, endorphin high and docile, as your other tit is grabbed and brutalized. The clamp comes down, steel chrome, cutting, and the nipple is crushed with quick, uncaring turns of the screw.

Shaking, shocky, you are about to start cumming until you pass out. The hands move away, and you are alone for a moment with your shiny, new clamps. That's all you can think … little slutty girl. *Ohhh fuck, ohh fuck, you know me, you know me.* The cock in your ass piston-pumps once with a remember-your-place casual sadistic shove that touches the top of your head back down to the grass. The hands behind you come back to your tits, and there is a chain. The hands are threading the chain between the clamps as you stare with dull, please-let-me-cum watery eyes before I cradle your face in my hands and kiss you, heartfelt and deep.

CHAPTER 8

Fingertip

As the fire burns in the fireplace, I open my eyes and look down at your head, before I glance over at the clock. Twenty minutes have passed. I listen to the rain coming down outside for a moment before I kiss your hair, moving my hand gently on your back. I feel you stir; your head lifts, and you look at me. I look at you, and we both smile. I lift my lips to yours, and we softly kiss; tender touches as we awaken, deeper kisses as we become fully aware. I turn toward you, and you move back onto the cushion, and we kiss—long, open-mouthed, make-out kissing. You feel my tongue touch yours and then my tongue in your mouth leading yours.

I pull away and kiss your chin; you lay your head back and offer me your throat. I ease back and place tender, soothing kisses, kissing down to your breastbone and then back up under your chin, before you feel my lips softly on your cheek and then my breath at your ear. There is a gentle sting of my teeth finding your earlobe. You moan softly as you feel my hand glide up your stomach and cup around your breast; the sting of soft, quick biting on your lobe and the sudden tightness of fingers finding your hard nipple, pinching it almost flat before rolling it slowly in my fingers.

Your eyes half close, and you breathe out. Your pussy begins to tingle and throb and juice, needing cock and tugging on your mind as you ease your hips toward me as you kiss back, hard. Your tongue finds mine, and you whimper quietly as I glide my hand down, flat and warm, and ease it over your mound. You are kissing and gasping as you feel your pussy cupped in my knowing, protective grip. You moan again, helplessly horny as you feel my hand press down on your sensitive, swollen lips. Your pussy screams out for penetration under the warm blanket of my hand. I press down on your labia with stiff fingers, and your breath catches. You shudder an exhaled breath as the ball of my middle finger traces slowly up and down your very wet slit.

Exchanging open kisses, tongues touching and exploring, increasing the heat of our bodies, you pull the comforter down and off. My lips go to your neck, and you hiss with pleasure, offering your neck and looking away. You lick your lips quickly and bite on your lower lip. Your pussy is puffy and swollen with the literal ache in your gut for hard cock, feeling the slow, measured movement of that fingertip on your dripping slit—sliding up, pausing, then down, pausing, then up. My lips, my tongue; you look into my eyes and run your hand on my shoulders. We're making out, loving it; the fire in your cunt burns hotter and hotter, stoked by the hand and that finger.

You turn your head back to me and look coyly into my eyes with a can-you-do-me-a-favor look of real need, an honest can-you-help-me look, a little embarrassed look of a woman who desperately needs to orgasm. I look into your eyes as the ball of my middle finger gets to the top of your slit and then goes a little further up to find the loose sling of your clit hood. My eyebrow raises slightly, and I hold your stare as my slick fingertip hunts innocently and playfully, dabbing and digging around, looking for your hard, hard little clitty. I watch your face get a sad look as your mouth opens; I see your breathless, silent, pleading moan and your body tightening, your eyes burning with sexual intensity, demanding, begging, pleading me to keep going. Keep going two more seconds; I'm gonna cum. The moment hangs in the balance, and my fingertip decides to head back down your slit and move away from your thrumming clit. Your eyes are misting from agonized frustration and disappointment before going back suddenly and completely to a tense look of impending orgasm, as my petulant fingertip reconsiders and returns to your throbbing clit nub.

I stare down into your eyes, reassuring and comforting you as you look up at me, staring intently. Your body starts to coil, and you hold yourself motionless as you feel the barest touch of the fingertip returning. You won't move; you promise you won't move. The fingertip touches on your clit and leaves and touches again like a butterfly—and you won't move, you won't move. Please ... please ...

Your eyes are squinting and closing and opening, glancing up at me and looking away. You struggle with the fingertip and the huge orgasm you feel is so ready to happen, as you offer a little smile at me. I see you are preoccupied with the effort of lifting your hips just enough, just a tiny amount, enough to get to the fingertip touching and hopefully— please, God—staying on your clit. Your whole lower lip goes into your mouth, and you are climbing a mountain, struggling, the huge cat-and-mouse effort of getting your stone-hard and desperate clit on the only game in town—that slick, perfect fingertip. *There, right there. I had it. Oh-God-yes-noooo, noooo, come back ... oh God, goddammit, God please.*

Your head is down, and I see your hips barely moving. I hear your exertion clearly in your hushed, heavy breaths and feel the soft bump of your pussy skin on my fingertip before I move it away again.

Your whole body is on fire now, every muscle tight, every muscle participating. Your mind and thoughts are down to cumming, and you feel my hand firm on your mound, everything but the fingertip, the part you need. Then it touches, and you hump-touch it back, but the connection doesn't last at all, or it lasts but not long enough. *There … right there … ohh God … yes, yes … yes … so close, so close, please, please.* You are right there, right on the edge—you need to cum. You look up at me suddenly with a painful grin on your face, and there are no words. It's so obvious you are about to cum, and you go expressionless. Your lips form an O, and you are on short breaths, and you are going to cum.

My fingertip slides away, and you realize it and look at me, lost and helpless and about to cry. I bring my lips down close and place a soft kiss on your lips. My stiff index and third fingers form a V and press your swollen labia down hard, pushing up your clit. My middle finger finds your clit hood and expertly lowers it to reveal and expose the nub of your rock-hard clit. My middle finger slides roughly down your juicy, wet slit and then comes back up to land softly, barely touching your clit. You look at me with wide eyes as you feel the ball of my finger go to the side of the nub and find that exact spot you like. You shudder and stare intensely as you feel the tiny back-and-forth strokes, and your whole body is responding.

My arm goes under your neck; your cheek is against my arm as I come down close and touch soft kisses on your lips and face. Your pussy is cupped in my hand, and my middle finger works your clit with a blend of sensitivity and roughness that takes your breath away as you feel yourself going over the edge. You feel your body coiling, your back arching, the orgasm blowing up and going to steel and then exploding, huge and sudden. You scream and scream out again and bite on my bicep and groan from your gut, each spasm jerking and screaming long and loud as your body is wracked by the second, and then the third and fourth orgasms. They explode hardcore and tumble over each other and wash over you, as you are cumming, cumming so hard.

CHAPTER 9

Delivery

You get in early, very early. Unlocking the front door, you let yourself in, flicking on the lights and getting to your desk. You place your coffee on the desk and sit down. Turning on your computer, you glance around at the empty quiet of the office for a moment before you turn in toward your desk and get to work. Later, as you finish, you look up at the clock and realize you still have an hour before everyone gets here, a whole hour. You sip your coffee and open some old files to look at.

The buzzer at the back door startles you, and you get up. The quiet of the empty office is all around you as you go to the door, eager for some company, even if it's only the delivery guy, Nick. *Oh, Nick, with your huge belly and your small talk that takes forever.* You sigh and open the door.

"Hi! Good morning. I have six cases of office paper for this address."

You stand for a moment, looking at me. *Nice eyes, nice smile; a crisp, white, long-sleeve dress shirt. Clean, well-fitting jeans and dress boots. Yeah.* You breathe out and recover and blink, your calm face on. "We already have a man who delivers—"

49

"Yes, you do. Nick. He called in sick this morning, and I'm helping out with his deliveries today. I'm his supervisor, Dennis. Nice to meet you."

The folded-back sleeve and the muscled arm, the wide hand as it comes up and you shake hands; the smile again as you are shaking hands. The feel of my hand warm and strong and the quivery twinge in your pussy.

"I have the cases in my trunk. If you'd like, I can bring them in."

"Oh, right. Yes, that would be fine."

I nod and smile, calm and confident and polite, before I turn away and start walking unhurriedly and purposefully toward the gray Lexus. You are staring at my shoulders, my back, my ass in those jeans, watching me as I quickly point the key fob. The car's lights flicker and the trunk pops open. I'm at the back of the car, bending over and leaning in, reaching with both arms and lifting out the boxes. Your face is calm, but your eyes stare as I turn toward you and begin walking back with the same unhurried walk, my arms loaded with cases. Our eyes happen to meet for a moment. It doesn't mean anything, of course, but if this was a bar and a Friday night ...

I get close, and you remember to turn and open the door, holding it open as I enter with the boxes. As I am looking at the door and concentrating, my shoulder grazes your chest in passing. It was unintentional, but you liked it; yes you did. You are right behind me as I get inside, and we both go down the hall to the storage room.

"In here?"

"Yes, thanks."

My hands are full. You apologize as you reach around me under the boxes to blindly find the door handle, gripping and turning it. The door opens, and your arm moves in with the door. The bulky boxes and my arm and body brush against you. You follow behind and turn on the lights in the open room. The door closes behind us. You stand by the table watching as I stack the boxes neatly, my back to you. You watch as I check the other boxes on the shelves and then as I bend over straight-legged to look closer at a label.

I straighten up and scan the shelves one more time before turning back around to face you. We are looking at each other again for just a moment. I glance over at the closed door, and you see the subtle change in my eyes. I come close to you, and our hands touch. You feel my hands touch lightly on your sides. Our eyes lock as you bring your hands to the front of my jeans; your hands come up and find the stud and undo it. I lean in and touch my lips to your neck, soft kisses and my breath warm on your ear as you pull the zipper down, down to the bottom. You fit your hand in, and your fingertips touch on hardness and skin. My kisses become more urgent now on your neck. As you ease your fingers in, you feel the warmth and the girth as you curl your hand around. My hands come down to open my jeans wide and tug them down as you ease my cock out, semihard and hardening, thick and pulsing in your hand.

My face lifts from the side of your neck to look into your eyes. Our lips quickly kiss, and you lower yourself down, your lips grazing my shirt as you go to your knees. It's all skin now, all muscled thighs and an eye-level bobbing cock, the dark of the slit and the two halves of the wide, purple head. You lean in and place a soft kiss on the slit, breathing in the scent of fresh-washed cock and the taste of precum on your lips. Your hands go wide and flat on my thighs, with my heartfelt moan far above you as you take my cock into your mouth, sucking slowly on the head before you take it all. Down and down, until you feel the head nudge at the back of your throat. You close your mouth and circle your lips on the base. Your mind glows, your stomach flutters and tightens, and your pussy is becoming a yearning, horny, wet mess. You press down a little more to get the head deeper into the back of your throat before you draw your head back. Feeling your lips slide up the hard bone of cock, feeling your lips touch and bump up and over the ridge and close gently as they leave the head, you kiss down the shaft and back up again, relishing, savoring, the veins and bumps and silky skin under the wet tip of your tongue.

You feel my hands under your arms, and you look up as you are helped up into my arms for a passionate kiss before I turn you with a firm urgency toward the table. Your fingertips touch the edge, and then your hands go flat as you are bent over forward, feeling my hands coming around and under and undoing the clasp of your slacks. The zipper goes down, and your slacks are eased back to your ass and then tugged down to your ankles. My hand presses suddenly and warmly on the damp crotch of your panties. You groan out loud as you feel my finger pressing the thin fabric on the length of your juicy slit, pressing your panties into your dripping, aching cunt as you hiss and cry out. Your head and shoulders go down to the tabletop, arching your back and your pussy slit pressing back on the finger. You groan again as I slide my finger up and down, slow and sure. Your panties are soaked and your hands grasping empty at the tabletop.

I bring my hands gently to your sides and find the thin band of your panties. Pinching on it gently, I ease your panties down. You breathe out, "Oh God," and go to your forearms as you feel the room air on your wet, swollen pussy—needing cock, needing cock so badly. You shudder as the wide head touches and then goes up and down in your wet slit. Your body tightens as your puffed and swollen labia open and close around it. Your arms go out wide, and you grip hard on the edges of the table. You are staring out at nothing. "Oh God, fuck me, just fuck me."

Your body shakes with raw need as you feel the cock head stopped at your hole and my hands tightening on your hips before your silent scream. The entire length of your pussy is filled and stretched by a hard cock that stays deep, by the sudden lunging muscled thrust that lifts your head and owns your cunt. The throbbing bone cock blindly touches the opening of your cervix before easing back. Feel the delicious pleasure of hard cock unsheathing from your spasming cunt in the moment before I use my legs and squat-ram my cock deep inside you. My forearms come down on both sides of you as I go to a slow, purposeful fuck. Your arms come in, and your hands find mine as you cry out in pleasure.

The top of the table is close to your face; your mouth is open, and your eyes are staring hard as your pussy grips and slips and your stomach tightens. Your breath catches and gasps out in low moans of pure need and total pleasure. The orgasm you've been missing and craving forever is forming, perfect and quick around the large male organ pounding your pussy to pudding. The hands at your sides slide under your chest and search, roughly finding and lifting your breasts, your nipples being pinched and rolled by strong fingers, and the electric current coursing through your body as your nipples are squeezed painfully tight. You groan loudly, the fence-rail cock fucking your quivering, surrendering cunt, marched to the very edge of a huge orgasm.

Chapter 10

Ridge

I'm laying you back gently on the bed, easing off your shorts, bending your legs back, gently spreading your knees. I'm looking at you with adoration in my eyes as I bring my face down and place soft kisses on the insides of your thighs, kissing down slowly until I am close, very close to your mound. I graze my nose gently in your moist bush and breathe you deep. I bring my hands down on either side and place my fingertips on your labia, gently spreading them apart as I point my tongue and place the tip carefully at the top of your slit, tracing slowly down to the bottom, letting the tip of my tongue play for moment in the wetness before going back up to the top. My tongue moves in tiny circles before sliding down your moistening slit, dabbing and licking at your juicy hole, before I flatten my tongue and lap slowly up your slit, roughly and rapidly. Pointing my tongue and touching at the bottom, I slide up to the top, running my tongue up and into the loose skin of your clit hood. My tongue is thick and wet and playful, digging around for your hardening clit before sliding back down. You feel my fingertips pressing gently and your swelling labia spreading apart a little more. My tongue eases in and slowly plows up and down. Your labia spread and curve around, as my thick, wet tongue moves up and down, up and down. You feel my arms tighten on your thighs and my tongue go all the way in, pulled out to the tip and back in deep, with slow, intentional strokes, flat-lapping at your slit before sliding up to your clit hood.

Pointing my tongue, I take my time, pressing very gently onto the loose skin and the bump of your hard clit, working the hood for a moment before easing it open, easing it down to expose your thrumming, hard clit. I lower the tip of my tongue very, very gently, resting it barely touching on the top ridge of your clit and then move my tongue back and forth, back and forth, barely moving, barely moving your throbbing clit.

Easing the tip of my tongue down the side, I find that spot you like so much—the tip of my tongue on the side of your clit, with the tiny back-and-forth stroking, rapid and controlled, and sending ripples of pleasure through your body. You moan softly, and I feel your hand in my hair. I bring my tongue back up and flutter the tip rapidly on your exposed and rock-hard clit, my fingertips working gently into your slit and pressing firmly on your swollen labia.

I move my head down and open my mouth wide, taking your pussy mound into my mouth in a single bite. My face presses down, and my lips seal over your throbbing labia and dripping slit. You feel my tongue everywhere at once; your back arches, and you press on the mattress with both feet. Bound securely in my muscled arms, you groan out and go back down on the bed. Your head is on the pillow and your eyes closed; your mouth opens and closes and falls open as your pussy is being eaten inside and out with lips and tongue and teeth. The spearing tongue fuck-thrusts, and the sucking pull of my mouth, the pinching sparkly heat pain of your hard clit between my teeth.

My tongue and mouth are suddenly gone, and you feel the air of the room on the wet mess of your pussy for a moment, before my arms tighten around your thighs and you feel my tongue back on your slit and pussy, harder than before. My muscled tongue dog-laps savagely and intensely, devouring your abused and overstimulated cunt. Your body hunches and tightens, and your orgasm rises up nut-hard and explodes. You scream out as your hips buck; your body wracks hard. No stopping, no showing of mercy; two of my stiff fingers are jammed up your tight, wet cunt, and you go over the edge again. The second, third, fourth, and fifth orgasms well up and explode, cresting and blending over each other. You have your head back, eyes closed, screaming out gutturally, and your body is on fire. The dog tongue is bullying on your rock-hard clit, and a third finger is working into your dripping, spasming cunt as a stiff pinky forces itself rudely into the tightness of your asshole—a slow pussy and ass fucking that wrings two more orgasms from your spent body before you collapse back, tears in your eyes, totally exhausted.

CHAPTER 11

Hallway

You walk casually down the empty hallway of the new geriatric wing, on your way over to the nurses' station in General to drop off the file in your hand. Your clogs are loud on the waxed floor and echoey against the fresh walls, but that's okay. There aren't any patients in this area until the end of the month. When you are reassigned here, you will get the standard rubber-soled shoes; problem solved. In the meantime, no one is going to hear you making a little noise as you shortcut through.

Slam!

You are suddenly staring at the wall, your face is against the wall and there is pressure on your neck.

"Do not scream. Do not fucking scream."

You swallow hard, your hands flat on the wall, the file you were holding down and scattered on the floor. My body is hard, pressing on yours, and you aren't going anywhere. Pulse racing, you breathe out hard as you feel rough breath at your ear.

"You were in the bar downtown last week … you and your girlfriends … all drinking and talking loud, talking about what got you off, and you—"

The sudden shove puts you hard against the wall, startles you, and takes your breath away for a moment. The whispering mouth is close to your ear.

"You said you wanted to get shoved up against a wall … get fucked. You and your friends all laughed, remember? Do you? Well, I was listening, and I didn't laugh. I took you seriously."

You breathe out slowly and nod, staying still, your pulse racing, your pussy tingling, your nipples hardening, the tightness and fluttery feeling in your stomach. The young intern behind you knows what he is doing; that chance hello at the hospital luncheon, those late-night phone conversations. And here you both are, meeting as agreed in this deserted hallway to play a little game—discreetly, of course.

"Please … no … don't … don't do this."

You feel my hands, strong and rough and rude; your smock goes up, and my hands go under, digging into your skin and finding the band of your pants. You are moved bodily as you feel and hear your pants being yanked down, down to your knees and then down again around your ankles. You are trying to say something, trying to form words, but it's all moans, and the wall is cold on your cheek. Your pussy is throbbing, and you feel the hands again; your thong is ripped down. Now your pants and thong are down around your ankles and bunched up on your clogs. You suddenly feel the cool hallway air on your ass and legs. You put your hands up higher on the wall and bend forward, pushing your pussy and ass back. You feel the first blunt shoves of cock head probing and missing, and you are so turned on. You feel your pussy juicing and dripping and your legs shaking. One more painful thud, and then your hole is found, and the sudden spearing of hard cock penetrates deep into your aching, horny cunt.

You lift your head from the wall and manage a hoarsely whispered, "Ohhh God" before your hands are sliding down and you are bending completely over. Your arms are straight and bridging to the wall, your head hanging down as the full-on fuck commences with a strength and intensity that bends your knees and blanks your mind. Your pussy cries out and surrenders and turns to mush under the onslaught of brutal cock strokes that pull your orgasm from deep within. You are over the edge before you can fully process what is happening. Your whole body goes taut as your orgasm explodes from every part of your body. You forget to breathe as incredibly pleasurable orgasms wash over you and you give up, you give in. You are squatting ass back into the ramming cock, offering your pussy more and more to the muscled huge presence pistoning between your spread legs. Your eyes fill with tears, and you cry out as the second and third waves of orgasms spark up and explode, intense and chaotic. You are a fuck toy now, a willing fuck toy riding a hard, thick stranger's cock in a deserted hallway.

Arms up, hands flat on the wall, your back is arched downward; your cheek and jaw slide back and forth on the cold stone as your pussy takes the brunt of the hard cocking and your body is shoved and pulled. You feel the cock slide out suddenly, and the hands on your hips are gone. Your legs are too weak now to hold you up; your hands are sliding down as you go to your knees. You feel a heavy hand on your shoulder that grips hard and spins you around, and you go to a sit, your back against the wall. You whimper quietly and open-mouthed as the hard cock appears in front of your face.

Whap! Whap!

The slaps hit one side of your face and then the other before going to rapid, deliberate blows back and forth. A hand has the top of your head, and you can't move your head at all, wincing as the cock club slaps hard on the hollows of your cheeks.

I step away, and you fall over to your side. With a surge of adrenaline, you turn yourself onto your hands and knees and begin to crawl, trying to crawl, your panties and scrub pants down and awkwardly binding around your calves and ankles. You try to crawl but barely start before you feel the hands again on your hips and you cry out. You begin the pleading, moaning, garbled pleas, but it's no use. You are stopped where you are. You feel the pressure on the back of your neck, and your head and shoulders are pushed down hard to the cold, waxy floor. The hands are hard on your ass cheeks now, and your cheeks are spreading apart. You feel your asshole as you dig your elbows down and try to pull yourself forward, but you are yanked back onto your calves and bunched-up pants. A moment of nothing before you are pushed forward and down, wincing and crying out at the blind stabs of cock hunting in the crack of your ass, hunting for your asshole. *Oh God, please not my hole. Please don't. Please, sir, not there, not there.*

After the briefest moment of contact, you feel the spongy hardness dead center and then the queasy, sudden stomach flutter, something pushing there and the impending insertion. These thoughts and a thousand others race through your mind, and your hands go out wide and slide uselessly on the waxed tiles. Then you feel the heat, the sudden pressure, localized heat stinging and the searing pain; hands painfully tight on your hips and the undeniable feeling of your sphincter being forced open. The ass-fuck, the cock suddenly sliding, filling your ass; your back arches even more, and your breasts press onto the floor. Your pussy is spasming and demanding hard fucking cock. You moan out loud as you push your ass back, greedy and needy; the humiliation and the abuse, and your mind is on fire, with the thrusting cock and your body coiling into another huge orgasm.

Going to your elbows and forearms, you press back into the hands that are pushing down, feeling the weight of my body enough to press your knees into the carpet, but no more than that. The closeness of my body, the feeling of the muscular and masculine, and the strength of cock deep, deep in your ass. The feeling of being under, of being pinned down. You feel my hands lighter now and the cock easing itself back. You go up to your hands and glance back with your eyes down. Your mind is seeing you as the prey, captured and ass-fucked. Your breath shudders out at the thought, and the thoughts keep coming. You were run down in the open field by the hungry man-beast and taken down, and your ass is his, his prize. With no time wasted, his rock-hard cock is buried in your ass. You feel cock sinking itself down deep, pulling up and almost out, then sinking back in much deeper. You feel yourself being pushed away and pulled back, made to ride the slow, plunging rail of cock and the sensations in your ass, the warmth building, and the pleasure tremors of a slow, deep ass-fuck.

Chapter 12

Relaxing

I place a soft kiss on your nose. Looking warmly and soothingly into your eyes, I bring my hands up to the front of your jeans. You feel me unbuttoning the stud, the zipper being eased down, your jeans opening, and my hands touching gently on your hips. A soft, quick, reassuring kiss touches your lips as I ease your jeans down, as you feel the room air on your dampening panties and the fluttery feeling in your stomach. My hands tighten slightly on your hips, and I guide you down to sit on the edge of the bed. You sit for a moment, look into my eyes, and lie back, lifting your legs slightly to help as I ease your jeans down to your ankles and off.

The tingling begins deep in your pussy. You breathe softly as I place a hand on each knee and spread your legs; your toes touch, dragging lightly on the carpet below. You breathe out hushed breaths as I place a kiss on each knee. I look into your eyes and nod and lower my lips to your thigh, giving soft kisses as I move up the soft skin, my face getting closer, soon only inches from the front of your panties. You feel your pussy swollen and needy and hungry; you feel the wetness of the thin material on your pussy and the feathery warmth of my breath on the other side. Your mouth is slack, and you are barely breathing as you stare down, as you watch me bring my hand up. I extend my finger and bring it gently forward. The ball of my finger touches barely down, stroking gently on the wet cloth just above your juicy hole. Your breath catches in your open mouth; your nipples are rock-hard now, and you swallow hard, your eyes intense. The soft finger strokes send shimmering pleasure tremors up thorough your body, flooding through your mind, as I look up at you with tender warmth.

I reach down with both hands and find your ankles. I lift your feet up and set them on the bed, flat on the mattress. Your knees bend and then open outward. You swallow and shudder inside as you feel my lips place a soft kiss on each side of the soaked crotch of your panties. Your head goes back, and your arms go out and away from your sides as you feel my finger and then your panties eased to the side. Your ass cheeks tighten as you keep yourself perfectly still, waiting and ready. *Oh God, please, please.* You feel the tip of my tongue, and your body bucks. You lie flat as I touch the wide tip of my tongue to the juices pooling in your aching pussy, biting your lower lip as you feel me moving my tongue around in tiny circles. You look up at the ceiling as I trace the tip of my tongue slowly and purposefully up your wet slit. Your swollen lips part and close around it, and you whimper quietly. The tip of my tongue reaches the top of your slit and pauses for just a moment, touching playfully at the loose skin of your clit hood. Your rock-hard clit twinges painfully underneath, and you hiss, sighing with need and mentally begging the petulant tongue to stay. You groan inside and coil with pleasure as I slide the tip of my tongue down your slit, quickly probing your hole before coming back up and fluttering rapidly on your clit hood.

Orgasms wisp and form deep inside you, as your body tightens and your hands grip hard and blindly at the sheets. You let out a heartfelt "Ohhh fuck," as you feel my open mouth cover your pussy mound and your sensitive, puffy labia are sucked up hard into my mouth. You suck in your breath roller coaster and let out a guttural moan of pure pleasure as I plow my tongue, thick and wet and warm, up and down your slit. Your back arches slightly upward as you feel the probing touch of a fingertip on your juiced asshole, a sudden focus and pressing as I ease my middle finger up into your tight ass. My tongue roots into your clit hood and finds the throbbing nub of your clit with expertise and works it knowingly back and forth—tender, bullying strokes that tighten the huge nut of an orgasm building rapidly in your gut.

Your jaw tenses, and you moan out loud as I slide my hands under and grip on your ass cheeks, spreading them roughly and piercing your tight asshole again. My middle finger goes in to the second knuckle as I hold you up and begin tongue-lapping your helpless, exposed pussy with muscled, sloppy dog-tongue strokes that cause you to shake with your coming orgasm. I harden my tongue and ram it deep into your cunt, your tight walls gripping as I go into a deep tongue-fuck. Your hands lift from the sheets in slow motion and then lower back down to grip hard as your orgasm balls up and explodes. You can't speak, can't form words; your pussy spurts a flood of juice, and your asshole grips tightly on my sliding middle finger. You lift and slam your hands down and scream out as the second, the third, the fourth, and fifth orgasms come on and explode on top of each other, intense and tumbling. You are moaning and screaming out, eyes tight, your head rolling side to side as the waves of pleasure overwhelm you.

CHAPTER 13

New Place

You're on your way home but running an errand first. The annual audit is being conducted by an outside accounting firm hired for the job, and it's going well. A folder was left behind, and you were asked if you could bring it over to the company offices on the way home.

"Sure," you said, "no problem."

The file is next to you on the passenger seat. You glance at your watch and see it's only been about twenty minutes. You are unhurried as you come down the boulevard and see the side street and turn. The road rises and takes you up into the hills a little ways, up into tree-lined, quiet streets and houses set back from the road, large houses long since converted to office complexes.

You find the address and take the long driveway into the property, arriving at the house a few moments later. You park in the graveled roundabout in front of the house, stop the car, and get out. File in hand, you look around for a moment at the thick woods and take in the quiet.

You look up at the house, find and confirm the number, and then go up the wide wooden stairs and onto the veranda porch. Stopping, you look around one more time before ringing the doorbell.

After a short wait, the door opens, and you are looking at a man about five feet ten, nice build; warm, intelligent eyes and a nice smile. You realize you have both stood there for a moment, saying nothing. Your eyes lock, and the sparkle in his eyes touches your insides. An entire conversation is happening—the words and questions and confessions and passing back and forth before you have time to even register what is happening.

"Hi. May I help you?"

"Hi … yes. I'm with the church your company is auditing right now. You or someone with your company left this folder."

You hold up the folder, and I lift my hand up to take it. Your eyes are on my hand and my arm and the jeans jacket—a little worn and comfortably broken in and fitting my muscled body like a glove. *Easy, girl, easy.*

The folder leaves your hand, and I am looking at the folder with those eyes.

"Oh! I'm sorry. You said one of us left this. Can you come in for a moment? Please, come in anyway. My manners suck. Excuse me again. Please come in. I just need to check something on the computer; it will just take a moment."

I step back and open the door further. You step inside, and it's very nice. Offices, yes, but in a homey setting that's both practical and warm. You look around the room and you look at me. I have the folder open, and I am looking intently at it. I look up at you and grin. "Sorry. Please, have a seat. I will be right back."

You are led into the living room, to the overstuffed couch. You have a seat, and I turn and walk out of the room. A hunk of a guy in a jeans jacket, a nice ass too.

Slow, girl ... just business. You sit back and look around some more, relaxing for the first time all day, letting your mind wander and smiling to yourself before putting on a serious face. You hold it even as your mind is putting you naked on the carpeted floor, on all fours and lowering your head and shoulders to the carpet, your hands gripping and opening and closing as you take my cock deep in your horny cunt. My jeans jacket is open, and my pants down, and that thick, hard cock is sliding in and out of your pussy. You cry out, and my hands tighten on your hips. I'm hard-fucking you now, reaming your cunt to a messy, wet mush with driving strokes that take your breath completely away as your orgasm builds, huge and imminent.

"All set. Just had to check a number. It wasn't me at your church today. Ted handled the call, and he left the file there, the dummy. I apologize on his behalf and for the inconvenience he caused you."

My hand finds yours, and you are looking down at it. My hand is holding yours and squeezing it gently and firmly. You feel your face burning hot; your stomach is flip-flopping, and you can't stop staring at the carpet, the thick carpet. Your mind is putting my cock in your naked, raised ass on that carpet and penetrating you.

Please stop thinking, please stop thinking. You feel the wetness outside your pussy now, and that's gonna show, gonna show so bad, so humiliating. Your mouth opens barely to a small O, and the orgasm is punching up your cunt and into your gut. You are right on the edge, right on the very edge. *Please don't, please don't, no please, no ... please no ... breathe, breathe ... ohhh, God ... okay ... good ... good.*

The crisis has passed. You realize you are looking down at my hand shaking yours, and you remember about shaking hands. You shake back and drop my hand, and that's that.

You have to go; you have to be out of here. A few polite words and gone.

"Oh! Sure, no problem. It was right on my way home. Well, a few minutes out of the way, but not too far, really. It's fine. I could come here every day."

You are looking at me, and you realize what you just said. You freeze in horror and embarrassment. I must know for sure now what you were thinking about. In the quiet of the empty house, you offer your hand again for some unknown reason, and I take your hand, and we are shaking hands again. You nod once and drop your hand and lower your eyes to the floor. You turn to leave, hoping I don't say anything about this to your boss.

"Hey! I … uh … shouldn't be doing this. We've bothered you enough already."

You turn around. "Yes? What is it?"

"Small favor? If you could bring this back and give it to Ted tomorrow, that would be a huge help."

You are facing me now. You see me standing behind the desk, and you watch me ease open the center drawer of the large mahogany desk. You watch me reach down, lift it, hold it up, and then flick it once, hard, as you feel yourself lifting your hand up and holding it open. You're barely breathing as I put it in your hand and you feel the smooth, warm leather, the black leather hard in your hand before I take it back and sit down in the chair, placing it down on the desk.

"That's Ted's riding crop. This was his old office, and now it's mine. I'm trying to get rid of all the junk he left in here. Teddy is—or was—big-time into horses, and I'm just going to assume it was his."

You feel the orgasm you barely contained before come instantly back, tight and hard and anxious to happen deep inside your cunt. Your legs go tight and start shaking slightly.

You smile at me and glance down at the black leather handle and the black leather loop on the end. Your ass itches suddenly and so badly, you almost reach back and rub on it, your ass insistent and urging and your mind demanding the sting of that leather. Your pussy throbs again, and your nipples push on your blouse.

"Is that what that is? I've never seen one."

You answer in a voice you know isn't yours. You were hoping for casual indifference, but you heard *submissive* clear as day, and you can only lock eyes with me for a moment before you are looking back down at the desk. There is nowhere else to look, nowhere in the whole world besides straight down at that riding crop, the same one you saw in all those videos, and now the real-life real one is right in front of you.

You feel yourself shaking slightly as you reach down to pick up the crop. You answered my question calmly enough, and you allow yourself the luxury, the strategic relief from looking into those calm, penetrating eyes. Your moment of recovery is completely lost, as your hand touches on the smooth, tight leather handle again, and your pussy throbs so hard, you bite your lower lip. But you can do this. Pick it up and say good-bye and let yourself out and be gone and thank you very much.

You hear a drawer open as you straighten back up, and you see me reaching into the lower side drawer of my desk. My hand comes back out, and the white of the rope in my hand hits the desk, a small heap of white rope, shiny, white, and coiled.

"And this rope … can you take it?"

You are holding the crop lightly with both hands and trying to be casual about it, but when I toss the rope onto the desk, your slightly shaking body tenses, and you are looking at the rope, staring at the rope. Your mind is racing; the fantasies are coming on hard and fast, and your ass is craving and itchy. My face is innocent and smiling softly, but there is more there. You think you see more there; there has to be more there. Your legs are shaking now, and you swallow, honestly unsure if you are going to reply or just cum on the spot.

You look up into my eyes, and you don't care what I see in yours. You'll just answer really quickly and pick up that rope and hold on to this crop and turn away and be.

I roll back abruptly in my chair and stand up, casual and muscular and calm and relaxed. The denim jacket hangs open. I am by your side suddenly. My voice is warm and calm, and you can almost feel my breath on your ear. You are shaking badly now, and this has to stop. You have to go; you have to make dinner.

"I asked you if you could take it."

You lean forward slightly, listening, breathing quicker, trying to think, trying not to think, your fucking cunt driving you crazy as I speak quietly.

"I have a confession to make."

You nod, a little too hard and quickly. *Get a grip, girl, get a grip.*

"That riding crop isn't Ted's. It's mine. And the rope too."

"Oh? Is that right? It's nice rope, I mean it's—"

"I don't own a horse. I'm a dominant. I use that crop on women. And the rope sometimes. If I need to."

Your throat is tight, your eyes watering; there's a tightness in the center of your body from your throat down to your tingling clit and throbbing pussy. Your voice is thick and raspy. "On women?"

"Yes. On women. I use that riding crop on them … on their breasts … nipples … on their bare ass."

"Bare."

"Yes, on their bare asses. The sound of the leather … the sting."

You swallow hard again and try to answer, losing ground quickly now to the thoughts and cravings, your body and mind on absolute fire. Hoarsely, honestly pained—shame and desire and need are in your whispered voice. "That sounds … wonderful. Sir."

The blood is pounding in your temples, and your hands are shaking. You can't look up from the desk or believe what you hear yourself saying. The riding crop is warm and black and leathery in your hands, and you can't stop. You can't stop the train now. Your eyes mist again from the confession, the intensity of this moment, and you need this. You need this so badly.

My voice is soft and very close to your ear, and your eyes close. "I was hoping you would say that. I really was. I assure you that whatever happens here stays between us; you have my solemn word. So if you want me to do this, to use that crop on you, I need you to hand it to me."

I am watching you as you sink down to your knees, as your head stays down, as you lift the riding crop with both hands above your head without looking and offer it to me. You offer the black leather instrument, already knowing and fully expecting it will be used on you. You're offering the crop and yourself at the same time—your head bowed, your thoughts racing, your pussy tight and wet, your whole body a sensitive, tingling clit.

I reach down and ease my fingers around the crop, lifting it gently from your hands, which stay up for a moment longer before you slowly lower them, unsure of what to do. You're barely able to keep up with what is happening. I place the crop down on my desk. I reach down with both hands and go under your arms, easing you up to your feet. You are trying to look down, glancing up with open, trusting eyes, doe-eyed and misty with frustrated need. This is it; this is happening now. Your eyes stay up and drink in the calm strength in my eyes, the knowing look that reassures you that you are wanted, treasured; your needs are natural and real.

My hands go to your shoulders, and you are being turned toward the desk. You are facing the desk now; your hands are going down and touching the warm mahogany. This is so real, so unreal; every detail is so sharp and clear—the top of the desk and the blotter and a pen left there, notes and a book and the riding crop. Your hands are flat, and you are staring at the crop. It seems so big on the desk, so big and shiny and hard and black, and you should go. You have dinner you have to make. Then you feel hands touching your hips and coming around to the front of your pants, and then fingers, knowing fingers. The clasp is being undone, and the zipper is going down. You feel the air on top, and then your pants open. The hands are guiding along the band to the back—*oh, God*—the gentle tugging and the pull, and your pants going down, over your ass and down. You feel your pants on your calves, and you feel air on your thighs. *Oh my God, this is happening. This man just lowered your pants.* You gasp, groaning quietly as you feel the fingers and your panties going down. *Yes, they're down, they're down.* You are bending over this desk in this office with this man, and your pants and panties are down. You feel the hand on the back of your neck, firm and warm. You are going down to the desk, your face to the blotter. The side of your face is on the blotter.

You are looking hard at nothing and breathing hard. Your hands go flat on the desk, and you are subconsciously bracing yourself. Your nipples are hard and throbbing and pressing hard on the desktop. Your breasts are flattened, your nipples so hard.

Thwap!

You move forward slightly, and your breath catches in your throat as the cold line on your ass cheeks goes red then white-hot. You feel the rush come up and fill you and go out to your fingertips and your pussy.

WhisssThwap!

Your upper body lifts your head from the desk, and it feels like a hundred feet up on a carnival ride. You are lightheaded and unfamiliar that there's a desk below you. Your head goes back down, and your face is back on the paper. Your feet shift, and your ass is exposed, so exposed; your pussy is so wet.

WhsssThwap! WhsssThwap!

On the other side now, pain coming from the other side of your ass, your other cheek; your ass-whipping in this office. Your Dom, your new Dom, whipping your ass with the riding crop you were just holding. *Ohhhh-fuckk-yessss.*

Your hands go slowly by themselves to the edge of the desk and grip it. Your ass is pure forest fire and your pussy a throbbing bloat of juice and labia. You are an old pro now; you can do this. This is what you dreamed of.

WhsssThwap, whsssThwap, whsssThwap!

The sudden bloom of searing-hot pain, the onslaught, the sound of rapid swats on your ass filling the room and your ears; you bite your lip and hunker down. The red sparkles in your mind's eye and the pain, the bright streaks of pain light up your nerves and your body. You are standing on weak legs now, leaning on the desk, hard and limp and trembling around the huge nut of an orgasm growing in your gut. It's growing from your fantasies, the orgasm you couldn't get with your fingers or your toys, coming up now, huge and hard and ready.

Ohhh, God, I'm gonna cum. I'm going to cum.

Then … nothing; no sounds. Only the smoothness of the crop gliding softly and gently over the angry red lines and welts. You shiver involuntarily, on the edge, right on the edge. You can't process anymore; you are ready, you are so ready, please, please.

And then my hand, soft on your heated skin, glides all over in big slow circles. It feels so good, so unexpected. There haven't been any words, any orders, any directions. *Thank you, sir. Your hand feels so good, sir. Please, may I cum now, sir? Ohh God, please.*

Thickness, two fingers suddenly slide down your ass crack, and you gag on the saliva in your throat. The fingers slide down as one over your aching, dripping cunt, down to the bottom, up to the top, and then back to the bottom of your slit, back up to your throbbing stone of a clit. Your clit is bullied back and forth, and then fingertips slowly circle over it, wet and sloppy, rude. Your legs bend, and your knees touch against the front of your master's desk. You are going to cum. *Please, sir, ohhh God, please, sir. I need to cum.*

Knees pressed hard to the desk, you are sliding yourself back, sliding your ass and pussy back, trying to get more of those fingers, that hardness. You just need a little more. *Please, sir, a little more.* Your back is angling down, and you are getting your dripping, horny, desperate pussy down onto those fingers. *Yes, right there, there, fuck me. Yes, fuck me.* But the hardness is slipping away, and it's gone, and you hear yourself whimper. You want, you need those fingers. And then you shiver; the lick touch of the leather loop feathers on your slit and swollen lips, the tap, tap, tap.

Thwap! *Oh, God, oh my God, sir. Please, no, yes yes, ohh-my-GODddd!* Thwap! Thwap!

The leather stings, fat and smooth and limp and sliding; the second right after the first and the third on top of the second, and it's time. It's now; you are going to cum.

Your forearms go down flat and deliberate on the desktop, and you orgasm, lost in the explosion of pleasure that fills your entire body at once. It's the total and complete body-wracking orgasm you've waited years for, the huge and magnificent and mushrooming layered orgasm that barely begins to end before the second orgasm hits you and then the third. You are on your arms, trying to ride it out, shuddering on your pussy as it pumps and juices. Your stomach muscles are tight and contracting. The orgasms come from your toes, so fucking satisfying. There are tears of real joy in your squeezed-tight eyes. You have found it. You are home. Oh, honey, you are so home.

Your arms go out straight on the desktop, the edge of the desk in your armpits, and you are down, squatting on your ankles, shuddering post-orgasm and trembling. You feel the softness of the comforter being draped over your shoulders, and you rest your head on your arm for a moment, recovering. You feel my hands on your sides, and you are being lifted, carried to the overstuffed leather couch. I sit you down in your comforter. My arm goes around you, and you lay your head on my chest and take in my scent. You feel warm and safe and loved, and you are asleep.

Friday, finally; TGIF. You mentally and automatically change "Thank God it's Friday" to "Thank goodness it's Friday" and then look around the office anyway before giggling to yourself. TGIF. The rest of the family going to the movies tonight to see that horror flick you just aren't into. You have the house to yourself and that bottle of white wine in the fridge. Oh yes, very nice.

You process the last of the paperwork from your in-basket and glance up at the clock—3:30. Might leave a little early.

The phone on your desk rings, and you pick up, introducing yourself as you tuck the paperwork neatly into the basket, thinking about the nice glass of chilled white Zin waiting for you at home.

"Hi. Glad I caught you."

You recognize the voice immediately, the events of last Monday fresh in your mind, having played them over with your Hitachi vibe several times. But this is the first time you've actually spoken since then, and you find yourself a little nervous, a little guarded. It was just that one time, ancient history, best forgotten. Not that you were really wanting that, but let's be practical about this; he's a big-time single lawyer, and you are … well.

"Hi." *Good, good … calm and professional.* "Umm … yes. Hi. How are you?"

"Fine, thanks. And yourself?"

"Fine, thank you."

There. Moment passed. Professional terms. Bygones be bygones. You are pressing the point of the pencil into your pad and biting your lower lip, but that's the way it has to be. Case closed, history, moving on.

"Listen, I'm sorry to bother you this late in the day, but I'm kind of in a bind. Ted left another folder at your business, and I really kind of need it. Tonight."

The audit ended yesterday. You watched Ted pack up his things. You shook his hand and thanked him, and he was gone, and there was nothing left behind. Nothing.

"A folder? I didn't see any folder; your guy Ted was pretty thorough."

"He left a folder."

You stare for a moment, the tone of his voice causing you to pause, going directly to your center. You turn your head away from the phone and breathe out, collecting yourself, trying to think rational thoughts but mostly grateful you are the only one in the office.

"Did he? I didn't—"

"He left a folder that I need, and you are going to bring it to me. You are going to bring that folder here to this office, because you are my slut, and I need to see my cock in your kneeling, naked, subbie mouth. Is that better?"

You curl forward slightly in your chair as your stomach tightens and your pussy knots and twinges like a ball of thick rubber bands being stretched and played with. You hear your pulse in your temples suddenly, and you feel your nipples hardening. You know exactly where you are going after this call. You swallow hard and squeeze your legs discreetly together. You just want to be there and out of these clothes, naked and on your knees, sucking on that hard cock.

You look at the phone and look around the office. When you answer, your voice has dropped very low, almost to a whisper. "Yes … yes. Yes, sir. I can bring that folder over to you, no problem."

"Tonight."

"Yes."

"Right after work."

"Yes."

"Like, now."

"Yes."

"Good. Drive safe. Good-bye."

"Bye."

You hang up the phone and glance around, and you are fine. You watch your hand find the mouse and click windows closed and shut down the computer for the weekend, like you've done a hundred times before, and you are done. You blink and snap out of it; you stand up and grab your purse, and you are walking out of the office, waving good-bye and saying, "Have a nice weekend." From anyone's guess, the vanilla you they know is heading home. Meanwhile, inside your very active mind and throbbing pussy, the real you, the too-often-denied you, knows where she's going.

You turn off the road and onto the driveway, down the drive with a little more familiarity. You arrive at the house, and the gravel is under the tires as you park, same as before; nothing has changed. You turn off the engine and get out. This time there is no folder to pick up from the passenger's side. You turn and face the house with the long porch and the wide stairs. This time you aren't the same woman you were last time. Your feet move you up the stairs, and your mind starts to race. You want to stop it, but you don't. Your darker thoughts are coming out, exciting and possible now. You get to the top of the stairs, and there's the door with a light on inside, just like last week. But last week the man inside didn't know a few things about you that he knows now, and you called him *sir* after he cropped your ass properly, and you called him *sir* on the office phone, and you are about to call him *sir* again when that door opens. Your stomach is tight, and your pussy is throbbing. You have it together, but you are so ready for this, so ready. You lift your hand and ring the doorbell, standing straight and poised, ready to turn and leave if this goes bad, if this was a mistake, if he laughs and apologizes and says it was only a joke.

The door opens wide and silently, I'm standing there with a nice smile on my face and warm eyes. "Hi! Great to see you again. Please, come in."

I step back, and you come in, passing close by me as you enter and look around, doing your best to look cool as you look everywhere but the office. Your dress feels transparent and incredibly skimpy as you stand there for what seems a long time, but you hear the door click softly closed, and you realize it's only been a few moments.

"So, do you have the folder?"

I am in front of you, sitting on the edge of the reception desk and looking at you calmly. You turn slightly to face me, and your stomach flutters. Your legs are tingly, and this is suddenly last week replayed. You have a folder to give me, and you are all "Nice to meet you. Here's your folder. Bye." You want that to be true and keep last week a fantasy, but your sexual self in that same moment rises up and takes over, and your vanilla self fades away. You feel yourself starting to breathe harder, but you aren't showing it. You smile, a knowing-the-joke smile. I look into your eyes and speak again. "You're right, bad joke."

I stand up from the desk, and I am close to you. My hands touch lightly on your sides, and neither of us is uncomfortable.

The smile is still on my face, but my eyes have changed. I am looking into your eyes and into your center with the same ease of last week, the same intention. You feel your lips part, and you breathe out.

"How about we head downstairs."

You have no idea what might be downstairs; you have every idea what is downstairs. The train is moving again, and you are on it, heading somewhere, toward something. You glance around the well-furnished and tastefully decorated main floor, with the desks and the bookshelves. Your gut and pussy are twinging, your hands a little shaky. The upstairs is so professional and acceptable, the downstairs out of sight, where secretly horny, pervy, submissive cock-and-pain sluts are taken and abused … abused—mouth, cunt, and ass—whipped. You swallow with effort and feel your breath a little jittery.

"Downstairs."

"Yes. A little more private."

You nod, biting the tip of your tongue, and you are calm. I take your hand gently and gentlemanly, and you squeeze mine, barely. The train is going full speed now, and the countryside is a blur. I turn and begin moving, and you follow just barely behind. There is no play here that you can tell. We go down a short hallway to a door. I open it, stepping back respectfully. The lights are on down there, and it looks as nice as the upstairs, from what you can see. You step forward and brush close past me, holding the door open, and you make your way down the carpeted and well-lit stairs.

You reach the bottom of the stairs before you giggle. You actually take another step and are standing near the couch before you turn yourself back to look at me, and I look at you without any indication I heard anything. I raise my eyebrows a little and smile, and you smile back.

"Well. Here it is. Not your typical dimly lit chamber of doom and gloom. We store a lot of our law books down here. Lots of shelves; a quiet place to read … or have a drink."

I have already walked over to the bar built into a corner of the room and gone behind it. I am holding up an expensive glass in my hand and looking at you. "Speaking of, would you like a drink? A beer? Soda?"

You shake your head politely and look away, your heart racing, unsure of what is going to happen next but feeling calmer overall. Dirty and dingy this definitely was not, with the low lighting provided by the lamps here and there, the recessed lighting in the ceiling, the big-screen TV mounted in the wall over there, and the bookshelves. These people have money, definitely, and good taste.

"Yes, the big-screen works … but only for sports."

This time you giggle out loud, and a sense of relief floods quietly through you. You feel like you've stepped back from the edge of something. Your fear of creepy, dark rooms and chains on damp cinder-block walls is for the most part gone and replaced at the same time. Your inner balance happens, and you are good, very good. Scared, yes, scared in a horny can't-wait-for-something-to-happen way.

"That's the kind of TV I like."

"Ah, a fellow sports nut! We do a lot of Sundays down here."

I come out from behind the bar, and I am carrying the white rope. A little unexpected, but not; a little familiar, but not. White and silken, coiled neatly in my hand. You are staring at it but not staring, and your heart is racing again, and your pussy is officially a wet, throbbing hole. Your thoughts are racing too, and they are going there. You feel your submissive self coming out, and everything is in that fluid, changing moment when everything vanilla becomes erotic. You bite on your lower lip and then don't, trying to look calm.

"I thought you might remember this."

"Sort of."

"Sort of. Great."

I smile and chuckle to myself, looking into your eyes as I approach you. You are looking back into mine, and you see the glint and the firmness and the sparkle now. The change in my eyes and the change in the room and the talk about sports and teams fades rapidly and long ago; forgotten altogether as I stand close to you and stop, lifting both of your hands with one of my own. I speak quietly, unhurried. "Can you hold your hands up for me? That's it."

You are holding your hands up, wrists touching. You are looking into my eyes and doing your best to look detached and wondering why, as you are really looking at the top of my head and really looking down at the silken rope going around your wrists in those neat rows. Around your wrists and then down your forearms, neat row after neat row, until a good half of your forearms are covered by the rope. You are motionless as I loop the rope one more time and knot it tightly. You test your forearms for movement, and there is none; snug, not overly tight, but definitely bound. You swallow hard, and you are shaking slightly now—the fluttering in your stomach … and your pussy.

I've stepped back, and I'm looking at you calmly. My hair is neatly groomed, and I'm wearing a white, collared, long-sleeved shirt; gray, pressed, expensive slacks; the wingtip black dress shoes. You are looking down at the shoes and making your way back up, taking in the manicured hands, the cufflinks, up the buttoned shirt and then to my face, the slight smile. Finally you are looking into my eyes again, and your stare is steady.

I step up close to you again, and my hands are on your front. You feel the fingers and the buttons being undone and undone and … done. Your blouse is hanging open, and your black lace bra is visible. I look into your eyes and smile, and you blush, feeling like a line is being crossed, but I reach up again without hesitation and unclasp your best sexy bra. It is open and hanging to your sides, and your breasts are exposed. Your nipples feel rock hard and aching and pointing. You glance down at them and bite your lower lip and lift your arms to cover before you feel the rope. My hands are gone, and then you feel them on the front of your slacks and the clasp comes undone and the zipper is being pulled firmly down. Your slacks get loose, and you feel them sliding off of your hips. They drop down to your thighs and then down to your ankles. You feel air on your panties, and they feel soaked. You shudder with embarrassment, and your thoughts are on the rope on your arms. You know I am going to touch your panties next, and you feel your face burning, bound and half-naked and standing in the middle of this room.

You breathe out and open your eyes and focus. You realize I am not around you, and you hear the crack of the small plastic bottle of tonic water in my hands as I stand again behind the bar. You watch as I take a long sip and put the bottle gently on the bar; you realize you feel a little thirsty yourself now but say nothing as you continue to stand.

I pick up the bottle from the bar and come over to you. I bring the bottle to your lips, and you open your mouth without question and take a drink of the chilled water. I take the bottle away from your mouth and turn away, and you almost whimper. You wanted to say, "Thank you, sir," so badly that you are about to say it anyway when you hear someone coming down the stairs. You glance at me and my calm face and then at the stairs and the same expensive shoes and slacks and suit jacket.

It's Ted. Ted from the audit. Ted who came into your office and shyly asked if this was the church office, and you smiled at his shyness and said yes. You stood up and shook his hand and took in his good looks and build and wondered for a moment what a fuck from this guy would be like, in your usual horny, never-gonna-happen daydreamy way, before you got down to business and showed him the files.

You can do nothing but stand there, calmly mortified and way beyond embarrassed. Ted barely looks at you, and then he is at your side and his hands are on you. His hand touches roughly on both your breasts, and his other hand is on your panty-covered ass cheek. You shiver as you feel his mouth, sudden and unexpected on your ear and then your neck.

"I get this ass first," he says.

For a moment, you think he is talking to you, his voice soft and calm and certain. For a moment, you are back in the office, and you are about to beg his pardon. Then you realize he is talking past you. You glance over at me, and I am sitting down behind the bar, nodding and sipping at my water.

"Of course, Ted. You claimed it last week. I didn't forget."

You look away from me and bite your lower lip. You bend your knees and squat bounce slightly as you react to Ted's hands roaming your body without respect, wincing and looking up as you feel your nipple pinched painfully tight and tugged. You feel the hard press of a man's hand in your crotch and the rude fingers searching and pushing your panties into your obviously wet pussy. There is a momentary pause, and you happen to glance down, seeing his hand go into his suit pocket and the smooth, brown handle of the buck knife opening by your hip. The blade goes under the band, with a firm tug as the knife cuts through. You stare down, unmoving and panicky, as your cut panties hang in two parts and your bare hip shows. He is over on the other side, and you feel the same tug, and your panties fall forward and down, exposing your drippy, pulsing cunt. You feel the room air on your ass, and you know your panties are down back there too; your panties are up only by the crotch, wet and sticking to your pussy. You look down instinctively to see his hand grab and yank, and your panties go down to the carpet. This happens so quickly, you are barely processing the cut panties in a wet heap at your feet. *My panties, oh God.*

You feel the hand in your hair, and your head is yanked up. You are staring into Ted's cold eyes for barely a second before his hand forces your head at a downward angle, and you are looking closely at the purplish head of a huge cock protruding from crisp dress slacks, a thick cock, the veins and the head and the slit jutting out straight and pulsing and hard from the zipper hole. The cloth curves around on both sides of the shaft. Your hair is yanked again, and you are off balance. Your arms pull out on the rope uselessly as you go forward, and his hips move slightly to adjust for you. You are down; your face is down, brushing down the side of the cock before you feel the painful sting on your scalp and your head going up, rising up. The wide head, the slit, the cock head is an inch away, and then hands are on both sides of your head, crushingly tight. You are going down to cock in your mouth. You feel it on your tongue, pressing down, the sudden painful thump of cock at the back of your throat. You want to gag, but you can't. The hands are so tight, your ears are pounding. The pressure-pain on the back of your throat burns, growing, and then the silent pop, and you feel it in your throat, cock going into your throat, your whole mouth and in your throat. You have a cock in your fucking throat, throat-fucked. The tight hands are moving your head, and the cock comes up, the head on your tongue and then to the back of your throat, and the pop. Your eyes widen, and there is cock in your throat again.

Bent over, bent forward you are taking a rasping throat fuck. Your arms are bound down and useless. His hands move your head up and down the shaft of cock, owning your mouth and throat. Your blouse is opened and loose, your legs shake, and your panties are cut up at your feet.

"I wanted to fuck her in that office. I knew this throat would be tight."

"I know. I know you would have, and then she showed up here, which was sweet for us."

"Fuck yes. Right to our door and down our stairs."

You are listening to the words, murky and clear, your mind trying to compensate between the calm conversations it is hearing and the brutal physicality of what is happening in your mouth and throat.

"I'm gonna fuck her."

"Right there?"

"Yeah. Haven't been laid since Tuesday."

"I hear you."

"Oh fuck, that feels good. A few more minutes."

"Ted, we have her for another hour. Take her into the play room."

"Yeah. Why waste it? Okay."

The hands move to the back of your skull, and in the next moment, your nose is pressing against the belly skin above his cock. You are dry-heaving in reaction to the sudden midthroat stretching from forced-down cock and the hairy balls on your chin. Your stomach is queasy and tight, your mind beginning to skip and go blank.

From a distance, you feel the pole of cock sliding long and pulsing from your hurting throat. The head catches on the insides of your lips before it is gone. You are falling forward and would have fallen down, but your head and face hit a chest, and you feel hands down on the rope. Your head is down, and you are looking down, dazed, watching two hands looping white rope around and between your wrists. There is rope left dangling down, and you see the hand grab the end and pull it up, lifting you to stand straight.

I am looking at you and Ted, looking at your dazed but sparkling and defiant eyes, your breasts round and full inside your open blouse, the nipples throbbing dark red, your stomach and legs and the white silk rope keeping your arms out. The length of rope is tied around your wrists and then goes in a single length to Ted's hand. You look softened by the abuse but not broken, shaken a little but aroused a lot. Your eyes are unsure but already knowing and ready for more. I feel my cock stiffen to rock hardness.

"Take her to the play room."

Ted turns and begins to walk. The rope is already tight. You are pulled forward and off balance before you start walking, your arms out and horizontal as you are led away.

Chapter 14

Workout

You are walking hard. The dots on the treadmill fill in one after the other until they complete the circle and you push the off button, slowing your walk with the machine. You're sweaty, breathing hard, feeling good. Your T-shirt is warm and damp at your chest, your shorts warm and damp in the crotch; your new sneakers are bright and comfortable. It was a great workout and a great feeling.

"How's the new treadmill?"

Your hands are on the support bars, still slowing with the machine. Your walk slows as I come into the room behind you.

"Oh, hi. It's great. Two and a half miles."

I am by your side, and I drape a length of white silk on each of the supports. You watch as I tie one end and then take your wrist gently and guide it forward until your forearm is resting on the support. You stare down as I begin the neat rows, starting at your wrist and moving back, covering your forearm.

"And you're barely sweating; that's great. And the incline? Did you try the incline?"

It's only been minutes, maybe five minutes since I came into the room, since the ropes were placed. You look up from

88

your neatly bound forearm, but I am already on the other side. You feel your head move slowly as you try to keep up, your eyes going back down to white silk rows before you look over at your other forearm and the rows forming there.

"Uh, no. No incline yet … just the running."

"That's okay; plenty of time to try everything. Using it is the main thing."

You are breathing hard again but trying not to show it, your pulse quickening and your nipples going rock hard under your damp T-shirt. Your eyes get wide as you watch and feel my hand glide over the rows, watch my fingers as I check for tightness. Your leg goes up and down; you didn't mean it to. Your stomach is tightening, and you are getting squirmy, your pussy a wet, thrumming mess.

"Yes, I agree … sir."

You voice is throaty and whispery now. You feel the rope as your arms try to move. You are standing now, but barely, so fucking horny you can hardly speak. I've moved behind you, out of sight, and in the next moment, your shorts are down to your calves. You feel my hands at your hips again, and your panties are yanked down. You feel them lightly on your calves. Your knees bend; you didn't mean them to. Your naked ass and pussy present themselves for a moment before you straighten up and then bend forward again. Your mind is racing, your pussy pulsing, and your horny asshole itching to drive you mad, as your eyes close for a moment and you bite your lower lip not to moan loudly.

The treadmill is completely still now; the display lights are still on and red, but you barely see them as you feel a hand on each of your ass cheeks, wide and firm and gripping slightly. Your ass cheeks are being spread by those hands, and the room air goes in your crack and on your wetness. Your asshole is exposed and stretched slightly and puckering, your dripping mush of a cunt parting slightly. Your knees bend slightly because you are trying to stay standing, but it's difficult. The ropes on your arms are perfect and binding, and you just need this, the submission, the cock.

My voice comes sudden and near to your ear, soft and firm and husky. "Yes, sir, you agree, sir."

My hand touches your lower back and then a single thick finger slides down in the wetness of your sweat, sliding over the pucker and then coming back and finding it, with a tiny back and forth, homing in. Then the cool, white, sliding, stinging pain of that finger forcing itself into your asshole, past your asshole, past the giving tightness. You groan softly with feeling, the thick middle finger up and large in your ass.

I plant my legs shoulder-width apart. You stare as I unhook my jeans, ease down the zipper. My jeans fall open, and you watch my hand go to under the band of my briefs; the band is on my wrist, and my briefs go down as I ease out my half-hard, hanging cock and cum-heavy balls. You bite your lower lip as you watch my fingers grip lightly on the shaft, watch as my fingers glide up and down the veined shaft before I cup my fingers under and guide the shaft to your mouth, touching the wide, spongy head to your lips and tracing back and forth slowly and lightly.

Bringing my hand up gently under your jaw, I squeeze gently and open your mouth, touching the purplish-pink head to your half-open mouth, watching your lips round as I snug the head. I push gently but firmly, to ease the apple head into your mouth. Your lips turn inward with the head before sliding out around, circling around the shaft as you look up at me, waiting for permission to suck.

I stroke your hair gently. "Is my pet hungry for her master's cock?"

My hand is under your jaw. I place my other hand on the back of your head, wide and strong on the base of your skull. My cock is rock hard and jutting straight out. My hand leaves your jaw, and I lower the hard shaft down, touching the plump, split globes of the head to your pouty mouth, and then pushing with my hips to get the head into your mouth. I feel your tongue underneath and the ridges of the roof of your mouth on top, as I place both hands on the sides of your head and lean forward slightly, getting my cock into your mouth another inch. Your jaw opens wider, and your cheeks curve outward as my cock stuffs and occupies your mouth. I hear your muffled moan, and I feel your saliva, wet and warm, pooling around my cock meat. My cock swells even more as I feel your breath whisper out from your nose and feather lightly on the shaft.

Holding your head in my hands, I move my hips, feeling along the back of your mouth for the opening to your throat. Touching and moving, touching and finding the hole, pushing forward with the controlled strength of my muscled legs, until the head of my engorged cock is snug in the tight opening to your throat.

My hands tighten as I very slowly push, applying pressure, holding your head in place. I feel your throat opening tight on the head of my cock, pressing, pressing, feeling the give, feeling the opening stretching. I groan out loud from the pleasure as I push with a sudden, hard thrust, and the head of my cock pops through. I grip your head hard and tilt it forward as I slowly spear my cock all the way into your throat, groaning with pleasure at the tightness, at your throat muscles gripping my cock shaft, the wadding of my cock head tight in the depths of your spasming throat. I keep pushing in until my balls come to rest on your chin, hearing your muffled moans and gurgling breaths for a moment before I pull back with my hips and slowly unsheathe my cock from your throat. I pop the slick head from your mouth, keeping it close as you draw in ragged breaths, and then getting the head back in your mouth and gripping your head with both hands as I ram my cock back down into your throat. My heavy balls bounce against your chin.

Balls deep in your tight throat, I pull out. Your lips lift and lower over the crown of my cock head as I slide back out. I reach down with both hands on your shoulders and turn you away from me. You feel yourself going down to the carpet, the side of your face suddenly on the carpet and your hands flat. Your elbows are up, your back arched, and your ass up; you feel a hand on each cheek and your cheeks being spread. You breathe out hard and hiss, shuddering in surprise and pleasure as you feel my tongue, warm and wet and wide, in your ass crack. You stutter out a whimpering, mumbled gasp as you feel my tongue on your rosebud, on your puckering asshole. I am tracing the tip of my tongue around and around and back, and you cry out softly and then groan from your gut as you feel my hardened tongue ease into your ass. You lift your head and lay it back down as I tongue-fuck your ass with steady, knowing, deep strokes. You feel your asshole relaxing and taking in my tongue, and you close your eyes, your pussy thrumming and getting mushy wet. You want more, you need more, you need cock. You mumble words and nod your head as you feel the slick ball of my middle finger pressing on your horny asshole and then easing in with confident patience. Your pussy twinges, and you cry out again as I sink my middle finger in to the second knuckle and then back out to the tip, inserting to the second knuckle and back out, easing into a slow, butter-churning finger-fuck of your tight ass as you hide your face in your arm and beg for more.

Your knees slide out and down slightly; your ass is up and pointing and spread even more. You squeeze your eyes shut and moan quietly at the pleasure, the thick, round hardness sliding in and out. Your master owns your ass with his middle finger, and your eyes get hot and misty. Your heart aches. Your master knows you so well already, and it's been so long. The finger slides in your asshole, turning inward and rolling outward with it. You swallow hard and begin to feel an orgasm building deep in your pussy as you feel me hook my finger and move my hand forward, lifting you slightly. You feel yourself lifting up by a finger hooked in your asshole, and you have never felt so debased, so owned. The orgasm is rising rapidly, but you feel yourself lowered back down, and the slow, deep fingering of your ass continues.

CHAPTER 15

Upstairs

I push back on my chair and stand up; I come over to you and offer my hand. You look up into my eyes and then place your hand in mine and stand up. We go upstairs to the bedroom. We stand together, looking into each other's eyes. I reach down to the front of your jeans without looking and undo the stud. You are calmly holding your stance. I ease the zipper down and open your jeans, tugging them gently down and letting them drop to your ankles. Then I take a step back, and you take a step forward, stepping out of your jeans. You feel my fingertips on your skin and then on your panties. You feel them float down to your ankles. I take another step back, and you follow. I place my hands lightly on your hips as I bring my lips to yours for a soft kiss.

I turn toward the bed, and you do the same. I press lightly on your back, and you climb onto the bed, one knee up on the mattress and then the other as you crawl to the center and lay yourself flat on your stomach. Your shirt goes down to the small of your back and halfway over your naked cheeks; your toned legs straighten and spread.

The house is quiet; we are the only ones home. I come to the edge of the bed, looking down at your beautiful body for a moment before I reach down with one hand and guide your leg gently over to point toward the corner of the mattress. I go to the other side and do the same, guiding your other leg to line up with the corner … I come up to your shoulders and lift your arm gently, straightening it and placing your hand in the corner. You softly sigh into the pillow as I come around to your other arm and do the same.

I step over to my travel bag, opening it and reaching in, feeling around for a moment before pulling out several lengths of white rope. I come back to the bed and hold them up; the ropes go straight and of equal length as they hang. I pick one and lay it carefully by your leg, laying a single length next to your other leg before coming up to both of your arms.

I return to your leg. Lifting up the length of silken white rope, I bring it down to the bed frame, loop it once, and tie it tight. I bring the two ends up to your ankle, carefully positioning the rope before crisscrossing in a neat pattern of binding overlaps, covering your ankle completely before tying the ends with a sturdy knot.

I place my hands on the weave and check for tightness. Satisfied, I move over to your other ankle and rope it to the bed frame. Going up to your shoulders, I trace my hands down along your arms, paying attention to your closed eyes and hushed breath as I bind each wrist with the soft, silken rope. My lips barely brush at your ear. You feel my hands on your wrists, on the rope on your wrists, checking. You whimper and moan again as you feel the soft kiss on the back of your head. You are ready.

I return to my bag and pull out the strap, the black, three-inch-wide leather strap. I hold it up by the handle and let the bow of leather hang, looking it over for a moment before reconsidering and laying it down.

I open the bag further and pull out the flexible cane, swishing it in the air several times, the thin red fiberglass bending in the travel arc and snapping as I pull it up—very satisfying.

I turn and come over to the bed. You feel me, sense me. You are tied, bound.

Helpless.

Your body raises slightly and lowers back down as you breathe. The room is very quiet. I am standing back at your side, gauging the distance, half bending my arm and bringing the cane up, moving my arm and the cane in line and bringing my arm down slowly. I adjust more on the way down, centering the red rod of the cane on the top of the curve of your ass cheeks, stopping less than an inch above your soft skin; paused, then bringing the cane down very gently … gently—hovering for a final moment, barely above. You swallow and inhale loudly in the silence, your whole body tensing as I rest the top half of the cane on the curve of your ass.

You feel the thin, light line of hardness, the cane lying across your ass. You swallow hard and breathe out into the pillow, and you realize with a sudden adrenaline-fueled dread that the cane is gone, the cane has left your skin. Your pulse is pounding now in your ears. It's gone, the cane is gone. This is it, this is it. You barely hear the whisper of the fiberglass whipping through the air before a searing, white-hot pain fills your mind and explodes over your body. Your bound wrists and your hands grip hard at the air, your body tenses, and you are staring forward wide-eyed. Your breath is stopped, every muscle contracted, in the pain aura that peaks and then recedes to the burning pain on your ass—to a stinging pain now. At least you can take a breath; at least you can think.

This time you hear the off-tone whistle perfectly in the same instant the pain explodes again on your ass. Your mind locates it, quantifies it, tries to isolate it away in the second before the pain aura blossoms again over you, and you moan quietly into the pillow. Your skin is on fire, and the twinge in your pussy is so sudden and hungry, you chest-press your hard nipples into the sheets and grit your teeth—so hard, they are painful … yes … yes.

The whisper whistle enters your mind, and you rush to focus before screaming out at the searing pain of the cane landing and slicing into your ass. You feel the instant endorphin rush, and your eyes are tearing in the bliss. Your pussy muscles clench, and your nipples are bullets; your body moves, curling, coiling on its own, reveling in the pain.

Breathing hard, you sink deeper into the relief of subspace. You feel my hand touching your side and then sliding under. You are being lifted up by your stomach before you feel a pillow being pushed under and you are eased back down and then lifted again. A second pillow is stuffed carefully under. You settle down again but hardly move. The ropes on your ankles and wrists feel tighter as you are stretched. Your back is angled up, and your hips and ass are high.

Your mind blanks as your back erupts in fire, the stripling whip stroke of knotted leather and the leather ends dragging over your welted back. Shimmering stars light the dark of your mind as the leather lacings of the cat-o-nine-tails bites and drags over your reddened flesh a second and third time, a fourth and fifth, and then a blur of brutal whipping that leaves your back a pain map of angry red lines and welts. Your pussy is a wet, thrumming, swollen mess pressing greedily and frantically on the pillows for relief.

CHAPTER 16

Blindfold

This is white silk—very soft. I bring the material up slowly and touch it gently to your face. It makes a very nice blindfold. Would you like to try it?

You watch as I bring my other hand under the strip of cloth and then move my hands apart, a length of the silken blindfold bowing between them. I look into your eyes calmly as I bring the blindfold up.

You see the fine threads, the whiteness, the light of the room on the cloth and then feel the soft silk and darkness.

You sit still, your heart beating a little faster; the softness … the dark. You feel my hands at the back of your head, know that I am tying the ends, tying the careful knot. You feel the gentle warmth of my breath at your ear, my quiet words. "Does your blindfold feel okay?"

I place a soft kiss on your neck. "That's good."

Another soft kiss on your cheek, and then after a pause, I graze my lips for a moment on your neck, under your chin. "I want you to be comfortable."

You feel my hands cupping your breasts, squeezing them, admiring them. You feel my fingers on the buttons, calm and sure, as I open each one, all the way down. Your blouse is open; your pussy tingles.

You shiver with pleasure as you feel my lips again on your neck.

"Is that more comfortable?"

You feel my hand on the back of your head, checking the snugness of the blindfold, ensuring you are in total darkness.

In the next moment, you feel my hands move down to your shoulders and then your blouse being removed. The cool air of the room is on your back and stomach; a quick tug as your bra is opened. Your nipples harden quickly; your pussy gets wet. You are half-naked, blindfolded.

You gasp as you feel the sudden, wet warmth on your nipple, the tug of my mouth as I suckle hard for a moment and then flicker the tip of my tongue over it.

I suckle on your nipple, sucking it into my mouth, tugging, stretching your breast and then releasing, switching over to your other exposed and waiting breast as you moan quietly. I work each breast until you are gasping, gritting your teeth from the pleasure, your pussy throbbing. Back and forth, my warm, wet mouth goes, teeth biting gently on your swollen nipples, dark red and pulsing.

You feel yourself being lifted from the chair, your stomach fluttering and your knees going weak as your hard nipples brush against my chest. You can't see anything; so exposed and vulnerable, so ready.

My hands brush casually down your sides; then you feel my hands, strong and sure, opening your jeans and yanking them down, my hands on your panties yanking them down to your ankles.

Before you can react, you feel my arms around you, and you feel yourself pulled forward, your naked breasts and stomach pressing against me—and the surprise of a soft kiss.

My lips graze yours. You feel my hands glide down your sides, a full kiss as you feel my hands slide over your naked ass cheeks, cupping them, manhandling them. You feel yourself relaxing against me, your pussy thrumming, your slit wet with your juices—so good.

You feel me bending slightly, my forearms going under your buttocks, and you are lifted suddenly and easily. Your jeans and panties fall away as you are carried.

Before you can think, you feel yourself being laid down gently on hard wood; you realize it's the dining-room table.

Still in the dark, lying flat on the dining-room table, you feel my hands on your shins, easing your knees up and then spreading them.

Your heart races, your pussy a warm, tingling, wet mound. You feel the room air and realize how exposed your cunt is, the puffy, swollen lips; the wet, juicy slit; the tender petals; and oh fuck, your hard, throbbing clit.

You lay on your back, naked, blindfolded, your knees spread.

You don't see the long lengths of white braided rope that I pull out, but you feel the softness on the front of your ankle and then around and back, and you shudder from the pleasure as I wrap the rope in neat rows up your shin and the front of your thigh, binding your leg to itself.

Without a word, I move over and bind your other leg in the same way, both your legs bound in white braided rope.

You jump in surprise as you feel the warmth of my breath on your horny cunt, lifting your hips instinctively to offer your pussy, and for a moment you manage to get your thrumming cunt to my lips.

But the moment passes, and you feel my hand on your wrist and the now-familiar soft yet hard feel of the rope binding, wrap after wrap, until you feel the gentle tug telling you that your wrist is bound as I tie the knot down on the table leg. A moment later, you feel your my hand on your other wrist, and you know you are bound now, deeply bound. With a nervous start, you realize you can't free yourself, but it only adds to the tiny stirrings of orgasm deep inside you, the fluttery tightening of your stomach, the juicy mess of your pussy, so ready for hard, thick cock.

You blink behind your blindfold, startled, my lips close to your ear. Softly, gentle but firm, barely above a whisper, you hear my words clearly in the center of your dirty thoughts, the center of your cravings. "I am now going to eat your pussy, sweet one, just like you've been wanting, like you've been fantasizing … like you need it. Is that okay?"

I place a soft kiss on your neck and then a second one, working my way down, a kiss at the base of your neck.

You breathe out, moan softly, as you feel my hand near your sensitive, tingling pussy. You feel my fingertips, grazing idly up and down, barely touching the moist bush, so close to your cunt. Just a little more. You squirm. I can almost hear your thoughts, almost hear you begging me to ease my thick, stiff middle finger deep into your aching, horny cunt.

I kiss slowly down to your breasts, feeling the coiling tension in your body, the sexual frustration. I press my fingertips into your moist bush, barely touching the skin. I make a V with my fingers and slide down the sides of your pussy, pressing the lips but not the dripping slit and then move my fingers up and down, massaging the puffy lips.

At the same time, I take a nipple roughly into my mouth, sinking my teeth firmly for a moment in a stinging bite before sucking it hard.

You whimper quietly and then moan out loud as you move your head from side to side, the only movement you are allowed. You bring your knees back, and your feet lift from the table, all in an effort to get relief for your thrumming, pulsing cunt.

I release the dark-red nipple from my mouth and lift my hand from your pussy. You let out a quiet whimper, unsure of what is happening, wanting my mouth and hand back.

I walk around and place myself between your legs, facing you. I place a hand on each kneecap, the only parts of your legs showing from under the tight windings of rope, and spread them apart gently. The white braided rope on both sides goes all the way down to your hips, down to the soft pink lips of your exposed cunt and asshole.

I kiss each kneecap and then start kissing down the insides of your thighs, soft, lingering kisses, until I get to the moist, warm bush. I breathe in your scent, delicious. I place my fingertips on each side and gently spread your pussy lips, showing your slit, glistening wet with your juices.

I ease my tongue out and place the tip at the bottom. Then I bring it up slowly, tasting you. Your slit parts and closes around the firmness as I draw my tongue all the way up, placing the juice-covered tip of my tongue on the clit hood, nestling the tip there for a moment, feeling your hard clit beneath the loose skin of the hood.

I glance up to look at your face, half-hidden by the wide blindfold, your mouth slack. "Tell me how badly you want me to eat your pussy." I carefully spread your lips apart a little more. Then I flatten my tongue and place the tip at the bottom and drag my tongue up, covering your slit as I lap upward, the juices coating my tongue.

I bring my tongue back down and begin to lap hungrily at the soft, pink wetness, slow, firm laps that part the lips, my tongue pressing between. I spread the lips wider and continue to lick, turning my head to lick the insides of your swollen labia. I feel your hips pressing your cunt upward. As you arch your hips up, I harden my tongue and let it spear into the wet tightness of your cunt. You groan out loud and fall back onto the table, and I follow you down, my tongue still inside. I begin to tongue-fuck, forcing my tongue in to the base, out to the tip, and then all the way back in. I feel your muscles gripping and squeezing as I work my tongue in as deep as I can. I leave my tongue in and begin to circle it around, feeling the tight walls and the warm juices. You cry out and moan, hissing, getting close.

I ease my tongue out. I bring my mouth up and place it over your clit hood, feeling your rock-hard clit inside. I press the hood with my lips, squeezing, releasing, as I listen to your deep, ragged breaths.

Using my lips, I ease down the hood, exposing the tiny nub of hard skin. I press the tip of my tongue down on it— gentle pressure—and then bring the tip back and flutter it lightly over your throbbing clit.

Then I press my tongue down on it, manhandling it, rudely working your throbbing clit hard, back and forth, circling my tongue on it as you lift your hips and moan. You scream out in pleasure as I get your clit between my teeth and place sharp little bites that send sparks of pleasure-pain through your body as you writhe and whimper, your hands pulling at their bindings.

I bite and nibble on your clit, the flutter my tongue over the hard nub, over and over until I feel you going still, your body coiling. You are so close; just a few more seconds.

I pull back, letting the hood close over your clit. You cry out quietly, upset; you wanted to cum so badly.

You feel my hands on your kneecaps; you feel your knees being eased back toward your chest and being held there. You feel my lips and soft kisses on the backs of your thighs, and you feel the fluttering in your stomach.

You wince and gasp as I place a soft kiss on the center of your asshole. You blush under your blindfold, even as you think of how you've been craving this. The softness of the lips, the warmth of breath; you feel your sensitive asshole puckering. You gasp again, electrified, as you feel the tip of my tongue.

I trace slowly around the tight ring, feeling every nook and ridge of your tight hole—slowly around and then back the other way. You feel me stop, then my hands on your wrist, untying the rope. You hear me walk around and untie the other wrist as well.

Before you can think, you feel my hand on your wrist and your wrist being moved to the side of your knee, your knee pressed a little further back, and then the feel of the rope, looping around your wrist and knee, binding them together. You feel my hands at your other wrist, binding it to your other knee.

And you are now trussed, naked, on your back, helpless, and so close to cumming, your eyes are tearing and your stomach is rock hard.

You let out a small gasp as you feel the soft kiss on your thigh and then my breath on your asshole. You feel your ass cheeks clenching and your asshole puckering, oh fuck, so exposed, vulnerable, so lewd, so dirty. You know if you could, you would be fingering yourself to orgasm right now; you are so close, the orgasm would be huge—if you could just get your finger down to your asshole.

You cry out, again startled, as you feel my tongue, the slow circling on your sphincter that is driving you crazy with the need to cum—hard. I begin to lap at your asshole, dragging my tongue loosely over the tight knot, letting the tip of my tongue just catch on the center as I lap, fluttering the tip of my tongue over it, teasing it, then more slow tracing around, gently probing the center, feeling your asshole relaxing.

I harden my tongue and place the tip carefully in the center, snugging it, letting it conform to the wrinkled muscle. I begin to probe again, gently testing, letting your asshole get to know my tongue. Then, holding my tongue in place and pressing, feeling the firm resistance, the reluctance, the muscle gives way as my tongue enters.

I pause for just a moment, letting your asshole accommodate me, and then press, feeling the tightness as I ease my tongue all the way into your ass, feeling the tight ring of muscle grip hard and squeeze as I get my tongue in to the base.

Your asshole plays with my tongue as you let out a long, guttural moan of pleasure.

I ease my tongue out, needing to tug slightly. I flicker the tip of my tongue over the pinkish ring of muscle, feeling it pucker and then relax. I stiffen my tongue again and spear it deep into your ass, feeling your asshole gripping it, trying to pull it in.

Holding your bound legs, I push you back slightly and then pull you forward. Holding my stiff tongue still, I feel the rim of your asshole sliding down to the base of my tongue and then back to the tip, back down to the base— your ass fucking my tongue as I gently rock you.

I ease my tongue out and then turn and leave the room for a moment before returning. I grab the ropes that are binding you and then slide you gently to the edge of the table. I reposition my arms around you and lift you gently.

Surprised, you wonder what is happening as you feel me walking with you, going somewhere.

You feel yourself being lowered onto your back, onto softness. You feel my lips on your ear as I whisper softly, in a caring tone, "A soft quilt for my sweet one. I want you to be comfortable when you give your ass to me."

Your body tightens with pleasure; you've wanted this, craved this—bound, helpless, fucked in the ass. *Oh God, yes.*

Your knees are back, your pussy and ass exposed and open—the natural way to take a hard cock in your ass. Your pussy twinges, your stomach tight and fluttery. *So fucking lewd, so right.*

You feel the soft hardness, cock head sliding up and down your wet slit. *Oh God, yes, stick it in, fuck me, fuck me.*

After several slow minutes, the plowing, wide cock head stops and slides down over the skin that separates. You feel the sudden, wet, rubbery feel of cock head on your sphincter, pressing for a second before sliding up and down, smearing your lubricating juices on the skin, then right on your hole, and then the skin. You find yourself willing your ass cheeks to open wider. You want that cock.

And then comes the sudden pressure, the focused heat-pain, and the feeling of pushing in. You moan behind your blindfold.

I position the head of my cock on your glistening, tight asshole, the wide mushroom head easily covering it and hiding it completely. With a careful but steady pressure, I feel your asshole resisting and then opening, slowly, reluctantly, stretching to accommodate the cock that is spearing itself into your ass.

My cock is rock hard, the head snug and tight in the center of your rosebud, the tip of my hard bone pressing on the ringed muscle. I press, and you drag in a deep breath, hissing, your teeth showing.

My legs are straight, planted shoulder-width apart. I place a hand on each side of your bound legs for support and then begin to lift myself onto my toes as I press harder. You mewl quietly and then begin to groan as you feel your asshole surrendering, the stretching sensation telling you your most private part is being violated—not by your smooth finger, not pampered and coaxed by your favorite toy that fits just right. You stare into the darkness, your mind trying to process the feeling of a thick, hard cock entering your ass. Holding your legs tight, pressing, I let out a groan as I hear the pop of my cock head going past your sphincter. I feel the delicious tightness of your asshole gripping the hard shaft. With another groan of lust, I use my full weight to ram my cock all the way into your ass. You cry out in pleasure and pain at the sudden feeling of fullness—my cock suddenly deep in your ass, my balls resting on the top of your ass crack as I breathe deep, enjoying the sensation and the lewd view of my cock deep in your bound and helpless ass.

I breathe out, taking in your beautiful face beneath the silken blindfold, your soft lips parted as you breathe as well, waiting.

Your feet are on my shoulders, and my hands press lightly on the outsides of your bound arms. My hips touch the backs of your thighs, and the tightness of your rosebud is stretched and ringing the base of my cock.

I lean down, bringing my face close to yours, and let my lips graze gently on yours. My heart beats quicker as you respond, your lips finding mine in a slow, deep, passionate kiss. Our tongues touch and dance in heated passion.

I lift my lips away and place a soft, lingering kiss on your nose and each cheek. Then I straighten up, repositioning my hands on the tight rows of rope on the outside of your thighs. I raise my hips, drawing my throbbing cock back carefully, stopping when I feel the head of my cock catch just inside your sphincter; you mewl quietly.

I go up on my toes, using the strength of my legs and my hips to carefully drive my cock deep into your ass, groaning at the pleasurable tightness sliding down my cock—so fucking tight, we both gasp.

Satisfied you are okay, I pause and sink in deep, drawing back and then impaling. I ease into a slow, pistoning rhythm, fucking your ass as you lay bound and submissive, squirming with the dirty pleasure of an old-school hard-bone ass-fucking. I push my shoulders and lower body through your spread legs, my elbows going down on each side of you as I bring my mouth to your breast and take the hard nipple hungrily into my mouth, suckling hard on the raspberry flesh. My hips rise and fall behind me, power-driving my cock deep into your ass, hard, raping strokes that send my cock head deeper and deeper. You feel the pounding fullness and your slick, slippery asshole gripping and sliding deliciously.

I bring my arms back from between your legs and slide them under your ass, lifting you, holding you in place.

Leaning down hard, my chest presses hard on your breasts. You hear my soft, husky voice in your ear. "I'm gonna fuck your ass hard now, slut, hold you tight. No hiding your ass in the mattress."

You moan loudly as you feel my strong hands gripping your ass cheeks, holding them up, subjecting your ass to a merciless pounding. My breath hits hard on your neck as I mouth and kiss, my hips rising and pile-driving my throbbing cock viciously into your slackened asshole, turning your insides to mush as you scream out in pleasure.

I'm groaning, my balls tightening. "Feels so fucking good," I mumble, lost in lust. "Take my cock, bitch. Take it." Fucking that ass.

Changing the angle slightly, I ram my cock deep into your ass, the muscles of my legs and stomach in sharp relief as I body-slam my rock-hard club of a cock into your hungry, grasping ass. I feel the suction of your gut taking it in, your pussy spasming and juicing as your ass takes the brunt of cock and demands more. A sheen of sweat glistens on our bodies, full-on fuck animals, mindless with lust.

"Take it, take my cock, you fucking-ass whore. Oh fuck, I'm gonna seed your ass. God damn it, I'm going to fucking fill you, bitch. Ohhh fuck. My cum-filled balls are rising hard and tight in my sack. Oh, shit. You'd better cum for me, bitch. Cum for me, *right now!*"

You arch your back and begin to curl and tense into your orgasm. I slam all the way in, crying out as my cock spasms and begins to spew thick loads of warm semen deep into your bowels. I hold you as you scream out in a tremendous orgasm.

Holding you, my eyes are closed, unthinking. I slowly piston my cum-covered cock in short strokes deep in your ass. You shudder and groan into my neck as you shudder again and explode into another orgasm, slowly pumping until you are totally spent.

Falling to our sides, we both suck in deep breaths.

Gently and quickly, I untie the ropes, tossing them aside. I pull the comforter up and over you as we snuggle, your face on my chest, my arms around you. I place soft kisses on your hair.

CHAPTER 17

Primal

You happen to be in the kitchen when you hear the soft knock on the back door. In response, your tongue touches behind your front teeth, and you pull down on your T-shirt as your pace quickens to the back door. I am standing there, and you unlatch the screen door and open it. I bring my hand up to the door and open it more as you step back, I come inside, and our eyes meet in the second before your back is against the wall; my arms are on either side of your head. We are kissing, and I pull my lips back. I walk into the kitchen, and you follow behind, passing by me to go into the bedroom. The moment you enter, you feel my presence behind you. My hands on your hips, you slide around in my hands to face me, and we kiss again, open-mouthed heads tilting in for more. You feel my hands go under your shirt and slide up the bare skin of your back. You are looking up at the ceiling as my mouth leaves yours, my lips on your neck. I am slow kissing and suck-biting on your throat, and you breathe out, your nipples rock hard and your pussy pulse-thrumming to a twitching, tingling wet mess. You feel my hands slide down and under the thin band of your shorts.

I take you, hands wide on your ass cheeks, my fingertips touching and grazing on your horny cunt. You swallow hard and kiss on my thick hair and my ear as your ass is mauled. Greedy and rude, my fingertips dig into your wet, dripping slit. You moan quietly, your legs weakening as you kiss on my neck. You feel my hands sliding up and out from under your T-shirt. My strong hands grip your shoulders, and I urge you down. Before you can respond, I force you down to your knees. My hand finds your hair and the back of your head as you kiss the jeans, rough kissing me on the bulge.

The hand moves your head before the hand tugs your hair and head back. You watch and stare, shaky and horny and obedient, as the hands come up and unsnap the stud. One hand and the fingers find the tab, and the zipper gets lowered, the jeans opening as it goes down. You touch your tongue to your lips. The zipper is down and the hands go to the sides, slow easing the jeans down. I am wearing no underwear, so the shaft skin and cock hair pulls deliciously as the jeans are yanked down. I watch you eye the thick cock, half hard, hanging bowed inches from your face, your gaze transfixed by the split hearts of the wide head and the dark slit. Your eyes follow the vein on the shaft; you stare back at the head and glance up at me, eyes hopeful. My hand comes down and loosely grip the cock you want so badly. The slow up-and-down stroking lifts the cock rock hard and thick and jutting up. The helmet head awaits far above your mouth, the ball sack and cum-bloated balls an inch from your lips.

Your eyes close, and you find the sack with your mouth and tongue. Licking, kissing, and mouthing the balls blindly into your mouth, you kiss the sack flesh before you are pushed away again. Your eyes snap open as you take hard cock across your face, from the left and then the right. The rapid strokes club and pop your cheeks; it's hard as it slides across your lips and nose. Your face lifted, you take it, your eyes once again closed. Your tongue out, you shamelessly beg for a taste and you are rewarded. You feel the head, apple fat, touch and then tuck snug in the opening of your slack mouth, and you suck suddenly and whore-greedily. Your pussy juices as you get your mouth cocked, and you feel yourself being eased back as you suck. At the same moment you feel the push and the head of the cock at the back of your throat, the shaft opens your jaws and your lips wide. Your shoulders touch against the edge of the bed.

The hand at the back of your head lowers you down to the mattress, the cock going perpendicular with the effort. The cock's spongy head wads tight and tighter in the back of your unready throat; you feel the muscled strength build in my hips before the sudden thrust as the cock head pops through and wedges itself down in your throat. You feel the tight slide of cock as it fills your throat, the balls splayed on your chin before you feel it coming back up and then out of your mouth. You choke and gasp and draw breath before the head is at your lips once more, filling your mouth. Your head goes back and you feel my cock against the sore spot at the back of your throat. Your back to the bed and your ass on the carpet, the hands tighten on your head before the sudden, stuffing thrust of cock stretches your throat condom tight. You surrender.

Your hands grip at the bedspread as the throbbing cock butter-churns slowly and unhurriedly in your throat. Your pulse pounds in your ears, your legs kick out from under you and straighten themselves. Your muffled, earthy groans please me, as does the sight of your eyes tearing up—before the weight lifts and the cock is unsheathed from your throat with a single unapologetic yank that lifts your head before it drops back onto the mattress. You look up at the ceiling, not seeing anything. You feel my hands in your armpits as you are lifted easily and roughly onto the bed. Your head goes onto the pillows as you feel my hands under your knees as I lift your legs. I bend them back toward you. With your knees close to your head, you feel the room air, warm and sudden on your swollen, wet cunt and puckering asshole.

Your eyes closed, you hear yourself whisper, "Oh fuck," as the hands slide down to the backs of your thighs. I press down and pin you; my fingertips reach for your swollen labia. I spread them apart, and with my tongue thick and alive in your cunt, you arch your back and tense. You stay there, the tongue humping itself deeper and moving around on the muscled walls of your cunt. You groan out loud and grip on the greedy tongue. As it searches, your arms go around your legs and you pull back hard, offering your pussy more. A hard swallow followed by a moan catches in your throat as you feel the press of mouth and lips on your juicy pussy and the sudden fuck-strokes of my hard tongue as it pistons inside you.

Your hands grip the sheets, and your stomach tightens as the orgasm forms up and at the doorstep. You are going to cum and cum hard. Your feet go flat on the mattress and you begin to push, to help your orgasm to happen. "Right there … right there … *yes!* … ohhh, God … there!".

You feel the sudden emptiness. You whimper out loud before you force your lips tight; the second scream muffled, you buck as the tongue goes flat and wide on your labia and juicy, dripping slit. You press your back into the mattress as the tongue attacks, your pulse racing. You are feeling *literally* eaten, the tongue, hard and muscled, laps sloppy and intense on your tender petals. You feel the first sting and a tug, and a second bite. Your pussy flesh is trapped between biting teeth, and you are beyond words. Your body tenses tighter, your jaw stiffens, and your breaths come harsh and hot. The pleasure spasms explode in your mind as your pussy is eaten whole and raw.

Your arms out, your body sliding back and forth on the mattress, you feel the sudden sting of teeth biting on your cunt lip, stretching it taut. Your pussy hole dilates, squirting out juice, desperate for hard cock, desperate to be owned by thick, hard cock. Your hands go into my hair and play with it blindly as your head goes back and you hunch forward, riding the orgasm welling up. Your cunt lips chewed and pulled and tugged, and then lapped by the flat hound-dog tongue at play. I'm bullying your cunt, and you are on a different plane. The orgasm comes from every part of you, every cell, every nerve ending bursting in your writhing body all at once. Your bent legs hang there, useless and forgotten, as your pussy takes it all. All of your focus is on the lapping tongue and face as you ejaculate, screaming low and gutturally. The tongue goes deep, and you cum again, the orgasm coming from your lower back and out to the tongue so strong it lifts your hips. You are done thinking; your mind goes only to pleasure, the third-fourth-fifth orgasms come crowded and rapid and tumbling and exploding and you lose count, your pussy soaking your thighs and my face and the sheets. It feels so good, so fucking good, the words stop coming.

And when you are orgasmed out, you open your eyes and breathe deep recovery breaths. You stare up at the ceiling, aware that your ravished puss hole was only the first course. You gave your pussy on a plate and the plate came back licked clean—and it was only the appetizer.

You look up at the good-looking guy who asked you if that was the uptown bus a little earlier. You locked eyes, and there wasn't going to be dating or courtship or any of that bullshit. There was just the extra moment of pause as your bodies turned in just that little bit. It was two pieces fitting together fuck-tight and right. He could have bent you over the rail right then and there, and God help us, you both knew it.

The small talk completed and the right boxes checked off, the casual-yet-intense exchange of phone numbers and more small talk took place before you parted. The call that night and the glass-of-wine date the next night. It was all good: fun conversation, laughs, and honest respect. The walk-in-the-park dates that only added to it all, and then, the late-night discussions that two mature adults can have, filled with calm and open exchanges that turned intimate and sexual (as you both wanted) and the sex, primal and honest (as you both wanted). The first time was great. The second time was perfect; and it was soul-mate good in a sexual way, the meeting of two like minds. After that, the hookups, the visits, the stop-by-and-fuck dates began. The pleasured moments were soft and raw, the unhurried times of intense passion left you both spent, satisfied, clear headed, and unencumbered by the demands of a "dating" relationship.

This was working fine, very fine, for both of you.

Now, as you lie back, trying to breathe after orgasms that were both twinge deep and comfortably unsettling, you lick your lips and watch your breasts rise and fall, both nipples hard, raspberry-red, swollen little posts. You feel a hand lay on the top of each knee; your half-lidded eyes look up to see the top of my head down close to your stomach. You feel the sweet, wet drag of my lips wander wolfishly over the soft skin of your belly, and your mouth opens slightly. You're watching and feeling the wolf moving up and closer; your body tightens. You are the prey. You will be taken, subjected to the hard cock and ravished. You will be my willing handmaiden, submissive to the veined cock and sperm-filled balls. Your tenderness will be offered and taken by the ramming cock, a treasured piece of you surrendered by you for the greater pleasure of a fuck the way your mind and body crave it.

Below your breasts, between your breasts, you watch the kissing lips and face of the wolf who commands you. The cold, animal calm of my lusting eyes staring into yours causes your gut to melt and your pussy to knot and juice. Your knees fly apart and wide by themselves. You're so ready for fucking. You beg for cock. My hard eyes own you, no question. You turn away as the wolf's lips touch barely, touch tentatively, and graze softly. Your heightened, excited mind and senses focus suddenly and totally on those lips touching yours. Yours is a flower, a rose, a tenderness offered in intimate space, yearning for the masculine, muscled cock and the pleasures to come. The arms, down on either side of you, claim you for the fuck, but it's those lips that consume you. The offer is naked and innocent in its desperate need, and you feel it all. You feel the burn of tears in your eyes as you lift your head just barely and kiss those lips. The story written and the movie made and locked in your hearts, unspoken forever. The sudden, open-mouthed kiss forces your head back and down; it takes your breath away. The arms move the muscled body away and back, and you are stare again as I position myself. I kneel between your spread knees, straightened up on defined thighs. You see the cock, and your swallow catches in your throat. It's a club, lewd and jutting and unapologetic, wakened and hardened and ready; Your eyes are spellbound by the sight of the dark, shadowed slit and the two hearts of the pinkish head. The shaft is thick. Leading your eyes down, fuck-tourist spellbound, you admire the curled bush and beneath the wrinkled skin, loose and taut, the cum-heavy balls swing huge and delicious.

The cock bobs by itself, the apple head dipping slightly and rising. With a glimpse, you see the vein going down the side of the shaft; you look down at the hanging, ready balls of the cock machine. By instinct, you then look down to your own body, at your crotch and your scented pussy, as do I. It is looking dear and tiny, your mound moist and vulnerable. My hands come up wide and cover your knees easily, your legs, shaved and cared for, moved out of the way by those hands and arms. I am lost in the suck-breath, thrummy pulsing of your pussy, juicy and needy and nervous. The hand comes down and grips the cock, pointing it downward. I point the head at your quiv hole, and I snug down. I'm huge and way too big for you; my body straightens, my hands jam your knees back hard. Your head snaps back, and your breath stops in the sudden, cool-white heat of the searing you feel inside. Your cunt stretches and surrenders and welcomes the cock like a smooth train. I'm unstoppable through the wet walls; your gasp is held up in your throat too as you feel the touch-tap of cock head at the opening of your cervix. It's unreal; the cock slides back, slick and thick, and your juices help the head pulse in and out to the edge of your dazed pussy, the pause barely a pause. The cock rams back in the same way and distance like it was nothing, and your mind is fogging; your mind is lost to hazy-fuck thinking. It's all pleasure now. Your legs are folded back, and your tight thighs and your pussy are offered up, taking the hard-fuck cocking you were craving so much, so fucking much.

The chest comes up and presses on your face before lifting away; the held breath is let out and sucked in. The cock plunges deep and comes back and thrusts deep again;

the muscled body over you is moving in controlled, lusting, fucking motions so familiar to you. Your woman parts, tendered under the onslaught of spearing cock. It is art; it's magic; it's poetry of the most primal. Your face goes slack-tight; your stomach tightens and curls, forcing you to hunch and hold as the male urge takes you with long-bore and punishing strokes to your cooperating pussy. You are put in your place, your mind flooded with pleasure blossoms and explosions that push primal thoughts. Your rational mind goes gently to the caring man behind the heavy-balled thrusts that are destroying your pussy. You give in—totally. You thrust your hips up and push your pussy deeper into the abuse as your craving mind cries out for more.

Your arms up and your hands on my back, your hands slide off as I pull out. I glance down and slip the length of my cock out of your pussy, drawing back until the head comes up and forces your swollen labia into an O as it pops through. It hangs, glistening and delicious and masculine. I grab your hips, turn you into your thigh, and then hoist you up, turning your lower body onto your knees. Your ass cheeks spread, and I marvel at your asshole, dark and wrinkled, tight and reddish. Your pussy lips below, you get yourself to your elbows, your back arched downward. You feel my hands on the bottoms of your ass cheeks and thighs as I spread your legs wide. I tease your cunt with knowing hands, displaying your cunt for my eyes and needs and cock. The head and shaft slap down, weighty and hard, and the baseball head slides down from the bottom of your slit to the hole because I want it to. The head is easily bigger than your slit, but that doesn't stop you. That doesn't ever stop you, does it? I mentioned it once and you laughed, your mind racing with our pillow talk and conversations as I enter you, balls deep in a single muscled lunge that barely gets a dismissive hmmph from me. Your mouth goes wide open on the pillow as you turn your head down hard into the pillow. You grunt and scream at the thick and throbbing presence of my too-big cock that is suddenly overwhelming your guts. Lifting your head, you scream out as the cock slowly strokes you like a freight train. I'm stroking out to the lips then down, down deep into your cunt tunnel, your vaginal advantage, your pampered pussy. The awkward boyfriend hard-ons and dinners and poems and jewelry rendered meaningless by the ruthless girth of the mean cock using up your pretty spaces as I pile-drive your cunt to useless whore meat. My legs straight and spread, my ass cheeks dimpling, my balls hanging heavy, desperate to unload as the cock pounds to new depths looking for relief.

Lying on your sheets on your back, your legs in the air and bent back, your knees touching and sliding on the sweaty sides of your face as you take cock, your pussy squelches. It grip slides on the fuck-pole owning the stretching depths of your cunt as the stubble of man jaw burns and fire-sting of teeth bites on your neck. My chest crushes your breasts down; your rock-hard nipples throb like firecrackers beneath the shoving overstimulation of a man sport-fucking the booty snared between his muscled forearms. You moan in deep response to it all—the arms and chest and man-sweat you lick from that stubbled face and the cock you secretly die for. Your body tightens as your mind is stripped away as you try to keep up with the primal carnal overload.

I grunt and lift my chest away from you as my massive arms glide down your female form. The hands go to your hips; your eyes open to see me straight up, stomach and thigh muscles flexed. You gasp at the sudden amusement-ride flip I use to reposition you face-down on the bed. Your tits press into the sheets as your hips lift. You feel my hands on your ass, browsing and groping and squeezing your ass. Under an expensive skirt and designer panties, I imagine your "office" ass—and all the attention it attracts. I imagine you walking downtown, your ass high above those riding boots.

Here and now, your stomach tightens. You groan and a hoarse whisper erupts from you as your cheeks are spread, as your fruit is split open and inspected. You groan again as you feel the hard thumbs probe at your asshole, your rosebud. You react to the sudden touch of warm spit dead center; your mind feels it and sees it. Your asshole is stretched oval, and the frothy spit coats your backside. You arch instinctively as a hard bone of thumb penetrates and samples you for tightness.

You press your face into the pillow, shuddering from the quick burn of your asshole stretching to accommodate me, pleasure surging through you. Your dirty thoughts and your dark mind focus only on the thumb in your ass. Your pussy bloats with horny juices, your back arches down even more, and your ass cheeks spread in anticipation. Your rational mind demands an apology, but your asshole betrays you. It grips my thumb, greedy and needy as it pumps up and down before it slides out—and is gone. The air in the room is suddenly cool again; my warm, wet tongue laps you in strokes both firm and gentle. As the tip of my tongue traces slowly around your sphincter, your pussy twinges, your stomach flutters and goes and tight. In response to the circling tongue tip, you grip the sheets. The tongue tip jabs at you and eases into your ass. You stretch forward and quiver as the pleasure, unfamiliar and delicious, pulses through your body.

CHAPTER 18

Drinks

As you go about your vanilla life, doing and saying all of the right things, you wear a mask. You look dismayed and express your disapproval in just the right way. When some other vanilla person mentions sex (or God forbid, something remotely kinky), you smile dismissively and the conversation moves on. Only you know about the flutter and tightness in your gut this sort of conversation inspires. You are thinking about what was just said, distracted. You look at someone at the other table; you want them to fuck you, right here and right now. You want them to make you kneel as they ease their half-hard cock out in front of everyone and slap your upturned face with it. But instead, you sip your coffee and stay hidden behind your vanilla self.

You go about your day, and your thoughts never stop. You check out bodies and bulges and breasts and asses, wondering what they do with them. You want to fondle and lick and get dirty with her … or him—or that couple over there.

At the crowded bar, we happen to come up at the same time to order a drink. We stand there for several minutes, watching the lone bartender serving drinks at the other end of the bar. You glance around; I happen to glance back. I happen to be looking at you; we both smile politely.

"What is up with this bartender?" I ask.

"Yeah, it's crazy in here tonight," you agree.

We chat for several moments, and then there is quiet between us. You are about to turn back around when I tell you my name; you smile and face me, and you tell me your name. Jokingly and politely, we shake hands. The bartender appears suddenly, and we order our drinks. Suddenly, neither of us is in any hurry to leave. There is that glance, that moment that happened the first time you looked back and saw me. There is that fraction of a moment when our eyes meet; it was all there, wasn't it? My eyes wait for yours, calm and knowing. When you glance back, you look right into my eyes, right into the cool, glinting sparkle. You feel naked inside, your stomach tightens, and your pussy twinges deep. You look away. You look at the bartender, but it is already happening. Some guy stood beside you, right behind you. Some guy with those eyes and that look; *he knows … he has to know.*

You reach for your drink. With a tingling hand, you lift your glass and take a sip. With a steady hand, you put your drink down, counting the seconds until you dare turn around again. You know I'm right behind you—but what if I'm not? What if I left? What if I was just being friendly? You turn around to look, and you look at me looking at you, staring right into your mind. We laugh, and you breathe out and smile—and look back into my eyes.

Watching the bartender working his way back down to the far end of the bar, you touch a fingertip to the rim your glass, your thoughts and pulse racing. You breathe out, short and quick, and then turn yourself around to face me. I smile a warm grin, and we giggle for no reason. We begin to chat, and our words flow easily. We are both secretly amazed, very pleased at how well this is going. By the second drink, it's like we've known each other for years, and each moment seems to pop and sparkle. We barely glance at the drinks or the bartender; the tingling sensation comes from everywhere, and at once, you feel your nipples, hard and sensitive in your bra. Your breasts are full and ready for my hands, and your pussy is prominent and throbbing in your panties. You are so thankful you decided to wear your pantsuit. I grin midsentence and keep talking. I can see that you are thinking about me and liking me. I envision you on your knees; as I am calmly ease down the zipper of my slacks, you touch your tongue to your lips. You watch my hand go in and ease out the thick, half-hard shaft and the purplish, wide head of my cock. I move my hand away, and it hangs in front of your upturned face, virile and masculine and sexual, the dark slit and the teardrop head halves inches from your mouth.

"Your place?"

"Sure, I'd love to."

You smile at me and nod; I know your room number. You leave the bar and walk calmly to the elevator; the doors open, and you step inside, alone, feeling the tingle thrumming in your stomach. You push the button for your floor, and you stare at the doors as the elevator rises. You breathe out and touch the tip of your tongue to your lips, watching the lighted buttons move. Your face is calm, your eyes casual but intense. *These are the countdown moments,* you think, *when it's all in motion, and it's going to happen.* In the quiet alone-time moments, you feel your vanilla-you fading and your cock-hungry slut coming out. The two of you pass in your mind, your vanilla, hesitant and embarrassed, comments, but you don't hear them. The truly sexual side of you brushes her objections aside easily. *It's game on,* you think. *No stopping now.* The bell rings, and the elevator comes to a stop, ripping you from your thoughts. Your mind elsewhere, you step out of the elevator and nod politely to the couple and older woman standing there. As you pass them to walk down the hallway to your room, your heart beats wildly in your chest, your body tightens and relaxes in anticipation; it gets itself ready. Without your input, you pass key the door, open it, and step inside. The door closes, and you are in a hotel room in a strange city, and you know it will only be a few minutes until there is a knock.

No turning back …

You check yourself in the mirror for something to do, feeling every way sexual and calm, the excitement more in your mind than in your body. Or is it more in both? You touch your fingertips lightly to the back edge of the room chair and bite your lower lip. You look in the mirror one more time, and it's all good. You hear the soft knock. You are ready.

CHAPTER 19

Together

You are on your back on the bed, naked; I am next to you, propped up on my elbow. I shower your breasts with slow, soft kisses, and you sigh as you feel the tip of my tongue trace around your hardening nipple. I sigh too as I take your nipple in my mouth and suckle it, with light nibbles. My hand, firm and strong, cups your breast as I suck. I draw your nipple in with a slow, suctioning pull before I release and do it again.

I stop and bring my face up to yours, pausing for a moment to look into your eyes. My lips find yours for a tender kiss. I lift my head away and look at you; at the sight of the knowing grin on my face, your pussy tingles.

Without a word, I lean forward and place a soft kiss between your breasts, hovering casually to kiss each of your hard nipples. Without looking up, I begin to kiss you with evenly placed and adoring kisses down your tummy, down, down your leg. As my kisses drift down, I gently spread your legs. Your pussy tingles again in the cool bedroom air, and you feel the wetness inside and smile to yourself. You feel my lips on your inner thighs as I move back and forth and work my way up. You feel me lift your knees and spread them apart. Your pussy displayed and exposed now, my soft, methodical kisses tease you to a frenzy as I get closer.

Your stomach is thrums with anticipation, your ass clenches and relaxes. Your pussy, wet and waiting, thrills at the sensation of my warm breath. My mouth must be close, so close.

"You want to get your fingers down there, don't you?" I whisper. You feel my words against your lips. "You want to slide them into the wetness, don't you?"

You feel the tip of my tongue at the bottom of your slit. You feel it move back and forth in tiny movements as I taste your sweetness. You breathe out as my pressing tongue moves itself wide and flat. Slowly, surely, it dances up the slit as you relax, letting the thickness of my tongue fill your slit. I spread the swelling lips; you shiver and groan quietly as the delicious drag of my attentive tongue moves up and down, gently. You spread yourself wide for me, and I repay you with even more. Your hand touches on my head and hair, and you moan slowly. The thin petals of your pussy are ravished and bullied under my increasingly aggressive tongue; you cry out as the tip off my tongue touches just inside the tight wetness of your horny cunt.

You reach down with both hands and grab my hair; you groan in delight as I sink my thick, hard tongue deep into your spasming cunt. You arch your hips up as I begin to spear your sopping pussy with strong, penetrating strokes. I feel your cunt walls grasp and pull on my tongue-cock as it fucks you deeply.

You are moaning out loud, your body beginning to tense and curl as the first swells of orgasm are forming—your heels on my back, you urge me deeper. Your hands go back on the pillows as I continue to deep ream your aching, horny cunt.

You feel me pull out; the tip of my tongue traces to find your clitoral hood.

You bite your lip and breathe out, your jaw tense as I touch around the outside of the hood. You gasp as I trace it firmly on the sides. I feel the hard clit hiding inside before I take the loose skin of the hood in my mouth. I press my lips and squeeze gently as I suck on it. As I tug it up into my mouth and release, I feel your clit getting even bigger, even harder. I release the hood and press the sides down with my lips, exposing the hard nub. I delight at your shuddering gasps; I barely touch it and then begin to feather the tip of my tongue rapidly and directly over and on your exposed clit. I flicker back and forth—and then stop. I press my greedy tongue gently and directly on your aching clit, letting the hard, sensitive nub of flesh sink into the softness of my tongue. I then change gears and manhandle the captured clit in a rough back-and-forth that leaves you on the brink of screams. You arch your hips up desperately from the bed before you collapse back down. My hands go under your thighs and come up around. My hands, on both sides of your pussy, spread the puffy, swollen lips.

You moan in pleasure, and I feel your legs relax into the cradle of my arms. My hands hold your juicy pussy open. I tongue your tingling clit and pull my tongue back to let the hood close over it. I take the fleshy hood between my teeth and bite down on it with tiny sharp nips that send waves of pleasure through you. In your quietest voice, I hear you beg for more with guttural moans of intense pleasure. Your hands tight in my hair, I bite down harder and faster and am rewarded by your curse-filled cries of pure pleasure as your clit is bitten, your clit is chewed on and devoured. Your arms and hands slam down on the bed at the strong-tongued dog laps and pulls and stretches you in just the right way, all of the sensations emanating from your pleasured cunt. Your hips turn, your legs bend, and your body coils and tenses frantically. I return to your clit and begin to work it expertly, finding the exact spot and speed as you cry out and orgasm. It lasts barely seconds; you ride on top of the orgasm that wells up from down deep and explodes over you.

I hold your legs firmly in my arms as you thrash and pull, your pussy immobile under my lips and tongue. I working both back and forth without mercy as you whimper in pleasure. You moan as you feel the second and third orgasms coming.

I look up, past your raised hips to see your eyes half-closed with pleasure. Your stomach and pussy both throb and spasm under my mouth and tongue, as if you were going up the hill of a roller coaster. I continue to tongue and tip-fuck your rock-hard clit. I stay in that tiny spot on the side (you know the one) … oh fuck … here comes three and four! The third? Oh fuck! The fourth? Fuck it; who knows? We've both lost count, Your mind is a blur as the next orgasm and the next explode from your gut. Your pussy is numb, sex-drunk, ready and begging for more. My strong tongue dives fuck-deep into your cunt. Oh fuck! You lose track of the pleasure: *clit clittonguefuckclittonguefucktonguefuck … ohhhh God!* Your legs held tight, you scream out and your pussy pump-gushes a thick load of sweet juice on the hard tongue jammed deep. Your cunt muscles grip and tremble as you recover.

As the tremors fade, I flatten my tongue and gently clean the tenderness. I suckle, open-mouthed, your swollen lips and glistening slit.

You feel your knees held and move back toward you, and you sigh as you feel my mouth and tongue leave the soft petals and begin to kiss gently down. You squirm with anticipation and pleasure as you feel a soft kiss on the skin below. You squirm a little more at the delicious fluttering on your stomach as I push your knees up a little more.

You feel the tender touch of my lips when I place a soft kiss on the puckered center of your rosebud; it's a soft, lingering kiss that feels warm and heartfelt and right; a shiver runs through your body as you press your back down and lift it a little into the sweet touch. I trace slowly around, caressing every cranny and wrinkle; around and around, my tongue and lips explore you. I change direction to learn and relearn each sensitive fold. I feel you relax; I feel the intimate heat rise within as you spread your cheeks gently to totally expose your treasures. With slow, determined strokes and one hand on each cheek, I gently spread you open just a bit more. I watch your sweet opening go oval and gape slightly. Excited, I stiffen my tongue and bring the tip close for a gentle, slow stab at the center. I feel your asshole tighten for a moment around the very tip; before I press in, I feel the give and then ease into the tight ring. I hear you moan with pleasure as your asshole tightens around my tongue and squeezes it, plays with it. I sink my tongue in deep, all the way to the base; I press my face against your ass cheeks, and begin a slow tongue fuck. I feel the grip of your tight sphincter, and I fight to get my tongue in. I earn the intimate taste with each thrust as I ease and ass-fuck you as your ring relaxes. My face pressed in, my jaw works furiously, my tongue slides in deeply—out to the tip and then in deep. I force my tongue all the way in, move it around in slow circles, and widen the circular motion inside as your asshole squeezes and works the base of my tongue. I feel your hands in my hair as you whimper in pleasure and press my head to your ass. My tongue circles, swabs, and fights the tight squeeze-play of your asshole as it moves along smooth inner walls. I press my face harder, deeper into your soft, firm cheeks, and my jaw muscles strain as I force my tongue even deeper into your hungry ass and lap up your delicious, warm, intimate juices.

I reach up between your legs, and your groan changes as you feel my strong, skilled fingers slide up between your puffy, swollen lips to find the pulsing nub of your clit. I work it with juice-slicked strokes.

The ball of my middle finger manipulates your throbbing clit as your wet slit clings and drags deliciously on the thick finger-shaft. With three fingers together, I press and firmly massage your sensitive, swollen labia. I hold your humming, pulsating mound deep in the cradle of my hand as I step you closer and closer to another stomach-tightening orgasm. I feel my tongue begin to move in and out of your spasming asshole; my hard, deep thrusts are met by your greedy sphincter's need for a hard fuck. You suddenly realize how tight your body is, and that awareness slams through you as a tremendous wave of orgasms builds in your cunt, your asshole, and your hips.

You scream out as several orgasms explode and flood over you at once, just barely aware of the hand that is working your pussy harder. You feel sparkles of pain as I shower tiny bites on the glistening tight muscle of your asshole; you go over, writhing violently and loudly as another wave of orgasms hits.

You collapse onto the bed, your eyes filled with tears. Your breath ragged and body totally spent, you welcome the darkness as you close your eyes.

You feel the soft kiss on the back of your neck, and you half-smile, half-grin. You barely feel my hands on your hips at first, but you begin to waken when you feel your hips being raised. You become even more awake as you feel the momentary brush of—cock?—on your ass cheek. As the mattress moves slightly, you realize I am settling in behind you.

Already and again, you feel the tingling and thrumming in your ready cunt and ass.

You half-open your eyes, barely breathing. You are so sexed but so ready; you feel the fluttering in your stomach and the stray and sudden twinges of orgasms already building deep inside your gut and pussy. You are so ready.

You feel the soft, weighty thump of balls and ball sack land against your cunt, followed by the smooth hardness of my thick cock shaft as it snugs down between your ass cheeks. You then feel my cock head on the small of your back; my chest barely touches you on your back as I move into position. My strong forearms move in tight on either side of you, and you feel the urgent, soft rasp of my breath at your ear, My hand moves the damp strands of hair from your cheek so my lips can place a soft kiss.

Your mouth opens for a barely-there sigh as you melt into me, your heart racing with tenderness and love. The moment is so intimate, so animal. You save the closeness as my masculine body and thick cock press against your wet, wet pussy.

I plant one more kiss on your upturned face; our lips crush together and blend in a knowing dance before I move away.

My muscled thighs press against the backs of your legs, and you become aware of the sudden touch of cock head at the bottom of your slit; I drag up to the top and down and roughly plow your swollen labia; it separates and curves, barely closing in the wake before being separated again by returning cock, up and down before the pause. My wide cock head stops in the center of your slit, and then you feel it: the sudden, spearing, unstopping fullness of hard cock that fills and stretches the tight walls. A groan catches in your throat; your legs and arms stiffen and your back arches as the cock spears all the way down with one lunging, forceful stroke that bottoms out and owns your pussy. You try to breathe, but the sudden emptying feel of pulsing cock as it slides back, makes that unlikely. You hear yourself groan again, and mesmerized by the urgent cum signals your pussy is sending out, you fall.

"Oh God … fuck me!" you scream.

Your hips slam back, and the sudden, excruciating pleasure of cock spearing again into your surrendering, desperate cunt is more than you can take. You lift your head and groan out in pleasure. The fucking has begun; as my thrusts ram you, I relax into a deep, purposeful rhythm. You shiver as my hands hold your hips tight; these are the hands that take you but never hurt you. I move your hips forward and back and ride your slick, tight pussy on a hard rail of cock. This is an old-school fuck. The veined shaft of my cock drills deeply. I withdraw to the head and pause just long enough before plunging in all the way, my balls and sack landing heavily on the soft petals of your pussy. You press your forehead into the pillow as you moan in primal bliss as I pile-drive my cock into the deepest reaches of your needy cunt. With rapid, merciless thrusts, I feel my balls lift and tighten. I groan through gritted teeth as my cock spikes rock hard; your swollen labia curve around the shaft, and my ball sack hangs below your wet, fucked-hard pussy. You breathe out, mewling quietly. Your eyes are closed. You are so beautiful, so sexy. I unsheathe slowly; the lips of your pussy turn outward as they slide back on the shaft as I pull out. I look down on the glistening meat of my cock, already stiff and ready again; it hungers for your ass.

I look at your tight rosebud in anticipation. I let the slick, hard shaft barely touch it; it twitches as my cock head bumps over your asshole. We both feel the pulse of my cock and the sudden slight tensing of your body. The pink mushroom head covers the tiny hole beneath it. My shaft is so thick. You twinge again as my cock urges in, centered and unrelenting. You groan quietly as your asshole slowly opens and then tightens painfully on the shaft as I ease all the way in. I take your ass in one, slow, continuous thrust. My hands are flat on the bed on either side of you, my muscled body taut above you as the throbbing hardness of my cock impales your ass. Only my hips move as I raise and lower myself into you. You feel the head catch just inside before it sinks back in deeply. We both feel the soft warmth of the tentative then ever-longer strokes. We are fully engaged— cock, asshole, heart, and mind. You moan out loud at the sudden intense blooms of pre-orgasm; your throat tightens and your mind goes blank. Your lower lip quivers as your cheeks blow in and out.

"Holy fuck!" I hear you gasp. "This orgasm ... oh my God ... fuck ... oh God, it's coming."

This is it; you're going to cum.

"Please ... don't stop please don't—"

You lift your head and drop to your elbows, your legs lost to spasms. Your ass grips me as your pussy gushes.

I fall to your side, breathing hard, and take you gently in my arms. With weary, satisfied smiles, our lips touch with kisses too close for words.

Chapter 20

Behind

Down on your elbows, you lift your head up and breathe out; your mouth slack and open, your face impassive. I can see that you are deep in concentration as you bite on your lower lip. You push back and hold, push back and hold again, and ease your ass back on my static fingers. I slide them in and penetrate your asshole. I reach in and explore here and there inside your ass, and it feels good, so fucking good. You feel your pussy get wet, the tingly twinges start deep down as you hear yourself whisper.

"More …"

Your head down and your ass up, you feel my stiff fingers slide in. You are tight, but it all gets easier as your rosebud relaxes. You feel them go in and out, and then you feel them stop midway. You feel them spread apart, gentle and opposite; you feel your asshole being stretched open. You shudder at the dull, hazy waves of pleasure that roll through you as the fingers, crude and rude and sexy, dance on the itch in your ass that is growing by the minute. It's a horny itch that needs to be scratched so badly. You lose yourself to the horny, growing need for you to get something in your ass.

I ease my fingers out and lift the throbbing shaft of my engorged cock; I lean forward and let it snug in the crack of your ass. The head touches the air above the small of your back; with my hand, I press my cock down between your cheeks, my ball sack on your pussy. You whimper and tense as I grip the base of my cock and slap the head down hard on your asshole.

Eyes closed, you turn away and just breathe. You turn your head and your lips on my muscled bicep. You swallow and continue to breathe out as you feel soft kisses on your cheek, followed by more kisses here and there. You feel the tingle in your swollen nipples and the hungry thrum in your pussy. You feel each kiss and all of the affection, and you are ready. Your pussy twinges, needy for cock; your hand goes behind my head, and you kiss on my neck. My hands are on your hips, your ass and pussy are exposed, and we both feel the thrumming in your stomach. I have one hand on each ass cheek; I squeeze each and part them. My stiff fingers slide up and down your pussy slit. You lay your head on the cushion. Your hands are flat and pressed into the cushions; you feel my hands on your ass and pussy and lower back. This is not the groping you usually get, you realize; this is something different. You feel my hands reach gently for your ass cheeks; you feel my hands squeeze and release, squeeze again and release, squeeze a third time, but this time, I hold the squeeze firmly. You feel your ass cheeks spread apart in a calm and undeniable way that sends that tiny flutter through your stomach. You feel the room air suddenly in your ass crack, on your asshole, and on your pussy.

As you feel my thumbs tuck in between your cheeks, you bite your lower lip. When my thumbs touch you with passionate intention and press gently and directly on your rosebud, your eyes moisten. Your asshole is slowly stretched, and a thick, delicious shiver runs through your whole body. You arch your back down and angle your ass up as the thumbs press in for more of that stretch. Your nerve endings are on fire and are sending out pulses and tremors. You feel the thumbs push into your ass even more; it's so lewd and so dirty and so sexy, you are biting on your lower lip and whispering urgently. I know the orgasm is already forming deep in your pussy.

I hear your quiet whimper, and I look over at your face; your eyes are closed. The look of concentration as you bite on your lower lip arouses me. You are so cute and frustrated and horny; your head moves slightly on the pillow, and I press my thumbs in, up to the big knuckles to open a tiny, dark gap in your asshole. I hear the hiss of your breath and see your frown in concentration. As you give me ownership of your ass, my thumbs embed. With the tiny gap between them, I reward you. I bring my pinkies in closely to your pussy and graze the tips on your swollen, sensitive labia.

You lift yourself slowly up by your arms, and your head tilts back. Your arms straighten, and I hear a quiet whimper as I press on your puckering asshole with just the tips of my thumbs. Slowly, I graze the tips of my pinkies on your labia and move the tips closer to each other. I graze slowly up and down your dripping-wet slit.

You keep your back arched downward and your ass up as my hands spread your ass cheeks wide, my thumbs on your tight, wrinkled, puckering hole. My fingers caress your juicy, hungry cunt, and you look down at your hands and the back of the couch. You feel my hands slide around, and suddenly there are four fingers from each hand down between your legs. My fingers stiff and together, I jam into your slit and pull you apart to stretch and open your aching cunt widely.

You groan loudly; in the next instant, you are steered off of the couch by the hands wedged in your cunt. You try to minimize the pain; you lift yourself and turn with the hands up and off the couch. You go down on the carpet, your hands flat, as the hands jam deeper. You lurch forward awkwardly before you drop to your elbows. Then you realize the hands are gone from your pussy; you feel me behind you, and my thighs bump and brush against the backs of your thighs. You feel the sudden all-at-once warmth of a length of thick cock laying on your ass crack.

You go down on your hands and knees, your ass in my hands. I draw my hips back and watch my cock slide down your ass crack. It bobs slowly; rigid and swollen and ready, I lean forward and watch the purplish apple head of my cock line up with the pink meat and black hairs of your cunt. I bring my hand up and guide the head down; I move my hips and legs until the head of my cock touches your dripping, grasping hole. My hands go around to the front of your thighs, and I glance down one more time at the thick-veined shaft of my cock directly at your pussy, the head tucked within the wet lips.

I grab your thighs and, without warning, pull them to me. I lunge forward and sink my cock deep inside you. In a single, violent, controlled thrust, your pussy takes my cock to the base as your head goes up and you scream out.

As I hold your ass back, tightly to my hips, I feel your tight, muscular cunt stretch and grip my cock. I'm inside you, all the way in, up to my balls. I ease out slowly back out to the head; your pussy lips bow around the head before I push hard and sink my cock all the way in again. I drag back to the lips before going into immediate, plunging strokes. I hear your gurgled scream as you go down on one elbow. In a flash, you collapse; your hands slide out blindly from under your head and grip at nothing. I lean into the fuck and go full-on, cock-boring your hungry, aching cunt as you hiss and scream out into the carpet.

Your fingers dig into the carpet, your pussy filled to your cervix and emptied and filled again by thick cock. Your pussy walls stretch and grip and get a real workout; it's the attention you have both been craving. It's your favorite vibe and fingers doing their best, but this is what you needed, really needed. You feel the first touches of an orgasm; it blooms quickly into a mountain. As the pounding goes faster, your ass slaps back hard; your mind's eye is watching the glistening pussy-juiced cock shaft, veined and focused and rock hard, disappearing into your aching pussy hole and reappearing over and over again. The beautiful nasty pole of cock disappears again into your cunt, and you feel it. Oh God, you feel it. "Here it comes," I say with authority. "Here it comes … you're gonna cummmm!"

You scream out from your lungs and your gut; your pussy explodes in a beach-ball, pure-white, wildfire orgasm that stops your breath in your throat. You stare with a pained expression of pure pleasure as you orgasm. You feel it in your legs and toes and fingers; you shudder as your gut tightens. It's muscular and mental and emotional; you think to push back on that driving cock, but it drives you forward. At the same moment, you drop to your face. The rug burns you, but you don't care; you can't think. Cock has never done this. Cock had never fucked you this hard. You cum again from nowhere; you bear down, pussy-juice spurting from you.

"Ohhh-my-fucking-God-I'm-sorry-I'm-cum—" you gasp incoherently, "Don't-stop-don't-stop."

Your elbows bent, your hands go into tight fists. You draw them slowly in as the last orgasm fades with a shuddering finale. You ride it on down until it is over. You blink your eyes and sigh a harsh breath and begin to breathe again. Your breasts are flattened between your body and the carpet, your back is arched down, and your ass is in the air.

Your thighs, damp with your juices, tremble. You feel my hands on your ass and thighs and spent pussy, and you half-expect me to fall down and lay down next to you and sleep and recover … but my hands are still on you. You feel them up around your ass, and when you feel them stopping there, a small part of your mind going on alert. Otherwise, you are calm and relaxed and satiated. You feel your cheeks being parted and the tap-scratch of fingertips on your asshole. You swallow and jump slightly as a finger finds its way to the center and presses and moves on. You tense again as fingers slide up and down your wet slit. With a short slide over the little bit of skin, you feel the sudden point-specific pressure and the familiar, queasy, fluttering feel in your gut as you feel the finger force its way into your ass. The corkscrewing finger works its way in, and you moan quietly. I push my finger gently but firmly in to the second knuckle, and I feel your asshole tighten on my finger. I place my other hand squarely on your ass cheek to hold you steady as I begin to stroke my thick middle finger in and out of your ass. With two fingers on one side, my finger and thumb on the other, and my middle finger extended and stiff, I'm butter-churning slowly in your ass. Your asshole is rolled out and turned back in, gripping tightly to my ass-fuck finger as I loosen you up.

The wide head of cock touches the center, and I press slightly. You are spongy, and I am so much wider; your tiny hole is easily covered. You feel a firm press of my cock that grows to a warming pain. My hands, tight on your hips, grip you firmly. The warming pain in your ass is now a searing pain, a stretching pain. Your tiny bud does not want to open to me. Why? Your mind struggles even as you give in. You push back against me, and you hear me groan. The silent pop of the head piercing through and passing into your ass shocks us both. You rise up and then go completely down as you feel your ass filled with cock; the waves of pleasure roll up and over you. Your hands flat and arms straight, you shove your ass back and there is even more cock in your ass, up your ass. All you can think of is the thick, hard cock in your ass.

CHAPTER 21

After Work

You feel my palm press on the back of your neck and then grip it. The mail you just brought in is forgotten; your body goes tight and fluttery. You breathe out through your half-opened mouth, and your arms go out as your hands go lightly to the counter. My whispered words touch close to your ear.

In a second, you take it all in: the fading warmth of the late-afternoon light, the feel of the kitchen counter, the strong hands of your man on your throat, and finally, the promise of your man behind you. You breathe out hard and quietly and suck in a breath; your heart races. You swallow, and you feel it go down past the hands to the thrum in your gut and your pussy. You are so horny and needy, and you have been all day. Work was so long today, an endless, mindless parade of people and coworkers and the bullshit, but you couldn't begin to concentrate. The only thing on your mind today was cock—and these hands on your body. You daydreamed and the itch came, the hard, tight *need* in your pussy. You smiled and chatted and laughed with everyone even as thick cock and your needy throat commanded your attention. All you can think of now is how much you want to be throat-fucked by me, to feel your greedy throat stretch around my hard cock. It's always in your thoughts. Here and now, my lips brush against your hair; you shiver and breathe out again, your body and mind slipping deeper. Then you hear my voice again, warm and calm. It's a whisper that screams that I know your most-private thoughts.

"How was work today?"

"Fine, we—"

You stop talking; you have no choice. You *have* to stop as you feel the soft kisses on your neck, in the spaces around the hands. You hear yourself groan softly, your pussy a tingling, twinging, wet mess now. You can barely think about work or what work was. You feel me press on your ass, on your ass crack, and on your slacks. The hands on your neck move slightly and tighten, and there is another kiss on the soft skin of your neck. The pressure is there again, and you realize my cock is already out and hard and against your ass. You breathe out with shuddering gasps.

"And what were you thinking about."

It was not a question, you notice. It was a statement. You feel my lips on your neck again and the warm breath.

"We had a lot of people in the store and—"

"Cock."

"It was busy and we had—"

"My cock. In your throat."

"No … ohh, God."

You are trying your best to continue this little game we invented between us. You feel the vanilla you in your vanilla world fade away fast.

The lips and mouth leave your neck, and the hands loosen their grip. You then feel my arms on your sides and my hands on the front of your slacks. With knowing fingers, you feel me loosen the tab at your waist. Slowly, I pull the zipper down, all the way down in one pull. Your slacks open, they hang loosely around your hips, but just for a moment. I yank them down, and you feel them around your calves and ankles. You become instantly aware of the room air on the wetness of your panties. Your legs are locked but weak, and you feel yourself bend over. As you lower yourself down to the countertop, you feel my hands back to your throat. In a flash, I pull you upright. The deepest part of your pussy screams for me. Your lips tingle, and your panties are wet. You feel my hands begin to tighten on your neck.

"Cock-slut."

"No … no … please!" You are whispering now, disagreeing yes.

The hands leave your throat and grip your shoulders, to force you down to your forearms on the counter again, for only a moment. The hands pull you back up and spin you around to face me. I look into your eyes, and you see me. You see my kindness, my adoration of you, and the sparkle I save for you—but you also see the glint of arousal, the hard glint of the dom who offers you everything. The quickly forming orgasm in your gut goes up to your chest and throat, and you can only stare back. Deep in horny need, you offer yourself, you surrender yourself. The stare lasts only a moment before you feel my hands urge you down. I push you down firmly; your knees bend as you go down. Your eyes take it all in: the neck, the shirt collar, the buttons, the open pants, and then the two halves and slit of the wide apple cock head, and the shaft and the veins and the hair and the balls. You feel the floor under your knees as you settle back onto your calves; you look up at me, before lowering your eyes to the hard pole of cock inches from your face.

You see my throbbing cock, angled up and jutting out, the shaft over the middle of your face and the purplish-pink head above your eyes. It's between your eyes, one eye on each side as you stare up at me, your face serious with lust. My legs straight and planted shoulder-width, I bend down and bring my face close to yours. I stare into your eyes, and you feel my fingers on your blouse front. As I unbutton each one, you take your lower lip in gently and bite on it as your blouse falls open. My hands are firm on your bra, and we both gasp at the give of the clasp. Your bra pulled apart, you swallow and continue to hold my gaze as you feel your breasts fall out. You feel your nipples harden in the air, and you moan softly. You shift your weight to get a hard fold of clothing—a seam, *anything*—on your aching cunt.

I look down into your eyes, and you look up at me, your eyes shiny with lust and submissive arousal. You can't help but be jealous of my hand as it wraps itself lightly around the shaft of my cock. You watch the then-loose strokes and wonder at the easy familiarity of it all. The hand slides down to the balls and up to the head; as you watch me, I can see your mouth water. I know your pussy is twitchy and juicy for me. Your puppy-wide eyes glance up at me and beg. With one finger extended, I touch the head, lightly and directly. You ask with your eyes, and I nod. You lean forward and tremble with pent-up need. You purse your lips and place a soft kiss on the head. As you lick and tongue the slit, you taste the precum. You feel my hand caress the top of your head. You whimper in frustration as you feel my hand grip and tighten in your hair, to ease your head away. I'm only inches away, but it's so fucking far away. You feel your eyes start to sting as your breath catches on your throat.

Whap! Whap!

Wincing, you remain still and look up at me with steady eyes in the pause.

Whap! Whap! Whap! Whap!

You feel your eyes start to sting; your pulse races in your temples as you kneel on the kitchen floor with only your office blouse on, hanging open and loose around your breasts. You kneel submissively as the hard nut of an orgasm persists in your gut as you take hard cock back and forth across your face. You blink and wince with each slap as the swollen club of meat whips across the hollows of your cheeks. The spongy flesh of the passing head smears precum on your nose and lips, and you wince again at the onslaught of throbbing hardness on both sides of your face. Your body is tight and ready to cum, but you don't let on. You show no sign; you keep your face upraised and passive as the cock-beating continues. Again, the taste of precum sizzles on your lips; you bite your tongue and hold your whimper down in your tight gut, your frustrated pussy swollen and laden with juices as it rides on the smallest of seams in your pants.

You are about to wince again, but the cock stops before it makes contact again. You look up to see the hand and cock poised directly in front of you. With my other hand, I reach for your chin. You feel my hand, warm and firm and strong, find your jaws and pry them open. You open your mouth for me—wide … wider. You look up at me and see the command in my eyes; your insides melt a little more, and you feel yourself slide deeper into your submission. My hand tightens more and your mouth is fully open; your lips stretch as your mouth opens wider. My seeping cock head commands your attention, and you can see the cum-heavy balls before you. You recall all the times you've sucked this cock, and you relive the memory of many times these the balls tightened, released, and filled your mouth with thick ribbon wads of delicious cum.

The hand tightens to a clamp on your jaws; you stare at me and breathe out of your mouth. Your tongue is low and down, your mouth wide open and waiting; your mouth is nothing but a cum hole now. You watch the hand glide up and down the shaft. It grips and glides, and you wait. You stare, blinking, at the hand as it works my reddening, throbbing cock and those balls underneath. You know that your mouth is going to be filled with cum. No one at work knows how much of a cock slut you are. You breathe out and lift the tip of your tongue to your lips. You are ready, ready to take this load.

You hold your breath and release it in short gasps, your world reduced to the cock head that is close, so fucking close. You can feel your heart pound in your chest as your knees slide slowly out to your sides by themselves. You try to get your hump-desperate throbbing cunt to the hard floor as the head and slit approach your mouth. Oh God, you feel cock in the air and in your mouth; in the moment before you feel the sides of the head catch on and push past your stretched lips, you feel my hand on your chin. I open your mouth wider than you could have on your own. Your mouth ready, I push forward into you. Your mouth is filled with cock, your tongue pressed down by the hard shaft. My hands fly to the back of your head, and you feel my hands press around your skull. You glance up at me, and our eyes meet. Your lips move forward, the stomach muscles and pubic hair come closer, and then the thudding pressure of cock head hits the back of your throat. It's way too big to go down; you try to breathe but that's not happening.

"Ohh God," you gasp. "My throat! Please slow down, slow down."

You feel the sudden heat and an intense pain in the back of your throat. I pull your head forward, unaware of the searing-hot pain you feel. We both feel the sudden, silent pop as my cock lodges itself deeper and deeper. You can't breathe; your stomach churns; your body tenses and reacts to the violation. You close your eyes and *will* your throat to accept it, even as your mind sets off the alarms. It blanks and shuts down; the panic is electrical. You pull for air desperately with both nostrils, but it doesn't help. The pressure on the back of your head isn't letting up. Your stomach churns and the pain flares up in your throat.

You know the rules. You try to stop your hands, but they lift by themselves from your hips. They rise to random places in the air as you try to signal, to wave off, to time out, but your head is pounding and your throat is spasming. *We need to stop; we need to stop right now.*

My cock disappears inside your throat. I see your hands rise up, and I look down at you. You blink frantically and strain to breathe. I see your lips a thin circle around my cock shaft; I feel your throat tight around my cock. Then I recognize the signs of choking, even as your dedication to my cock moves me, and I can't let you down. I hold your head tightly and go to my toes. I use the strength of both legs, and pull your head forward with a brutal tug as I quarterback-ram my cock home. My heels off the floor, I lose my stability for a moment before I regain control. I go into a rough ride your face and throat, even as your hands go up and out and slap weakly on my thighs. Your muffled, gurgling fight to breathe and your wide, pleading eyes only add to my enjoyment. As I move your head on my cock, I feel my balls lift and tighten. My cock throbs and swells with nowhere to go in the stretched-to-the-limit muscled tightness of your throat. You buck wildly and try to go to one knee, but I hang on. I keep your head tight to my hips and your face to my hairs; I feel my balls starting to spasm, and I step forward. I push you back and get you between my legs. I hold you up from the floor by your head, and I groan out loud as I feel the spiking orgasm. I cum—hard. My jaw tight, I feel my balls pump and constrict painfully. I look down but then have to look up at the ceiling; the sensation of pumping my load directly into your stomach is so pleasurable, I keep my cock deep in your throat until I am completely spent. My cock and emptied balls still spasm as I reluctantly pull my softening cock from your throat, and ease you—shaking and breathless—to the kitchen floor.

Catching my breath, I lift you gently up into my arms, your head to my chest. I carry you into the living room and ease you onto the couch. I leave the room and come back a few minutes later with two glasses of chilled white wine. As I sit down next to you, I hand you one of them. I pull the comforter around us both, and we snuggle for a moment. I touch my glass to yours, and we both take a sip. You look at me; I put both of our glasses down and settle back. You put your head on my chest again, and I place a gentle kiss on your hair, the fire in the fireplace cheery and warm as we sit and relax.

Chapter 22

Lunch

I'm naked as I stand at the grill, tending to your lunch, your salad and plate near me on the counter. You see the thin straps of the apron strings tied in a bow on the small of my back, as well as the base of the butt plug nestled between the muscled cheeks of my ass. This puts you instantly in the mood; your pulse rises pleasantly with the familiar flutter of hunger in your gut that has nothing to do with the gourmet lunch being prepared for you. You lick your lips and smile to yourself as your pussy begs for some lunchtime cock. You nod to yourself from the doorway as you watch me work.

You come up behind me casually and plant a gentle kiss at the base of my neck. I continue to work, even as I feel your smooth hand on my back. Your cool hand trails slowly down, and I say nothing. I know not to speak when Mistress is playing. I touch at the chicken and add spices. My jaw tenses at the touch of your hand down there. I'm very close, and I move my legs further apart and plant my feet. I lift up slightly on my toes and ease my ass back, presenting just as you like it. I bite my lip and continue to cook. I hold position as I feel your playful tug on the plug, and then the quick tapping of your fingertip on the base. Your hands go to my hips and glide up my sides. At the sudden touch of the wet warmth of your pussy on my muscled thigh, I swallow hard. I no longer see the chicken; the only thing I am aware of is the gentle sliding pressure of your body as you move yourself up and down on mine. My cock goes rock hard under the apron before you slow and stop, before you rise and pause, before you go over to your chair.

I place the chicken on the plate with the salad and bring it over to you. You are seated on the counter, your legs spread wide for me. I see you smile at me and then glance down at my apron, tented up over my obvious erection. I approach, your plate in my hands. You take the plate from me with one hand, and I hand you your fork with the other. You look down at the plate now and touch at the salad with your fork. I go down, crouch level with your pussy, and bring my face close between your legs. I place a soft kiss on your moist slit, and flicker my tongue rapidly up and down. I hear you moan softly above me as I flatten my tongue and begin to lap gently.

You place the plate down, and I look up.

"I'm glad you are enjoying your lunch," I hear you say.

I look deeply into your eyes as I stand and bring my face close to yours, then closer. Our foreheads touch, my eyes locked on yours. I tilt my head and kiss you with a hard passion. Barely restrained, I pull away and look at you before I shower urgent kisses on your neck. With both hands, I pull your skirt out from under your ass, I hike up the back of your skirt and slide my hands on your ass cheeks and panties. I rock you side to side so I can yank those panties down. You feel the cool smoothness of the counter and then my hands as they move under your thighs into your crotch. My fingers and fingertips touch your moist, sweet cunt, and I kiss you—hard.

I have you, I have my prey. I have my woman. You groan into my neck and press yourself down on the fingers working your juicy, swollen pussy. You look into my eyes with genuine need, and I feel a surge in my cock and balls. I feel my mind on you in total focus; I feel the rush of adrenaline and lust for you rise up and flood over me. I have to have you, and you have to be naked, right now. I grab at the front of your blouse and pull it apart in a single motion that leaves your blouse loose and dangling. I pull it off your shoulders, and it falls to the counter. My hand reaches behind you; your bra is pulled tautly away before I let it snap back and apart. My hands swipe at your chest, and I yank your bra off your body. I grab-lift you, your breasts to my mouth. I hold you tight as I suckle and bite on your nipple fruit. Easing you down to your back on the counter, I scoop up your legs and get them over my shoulders. My hands, on the small of your back, lift your ass cheeks. I get my face back down and attack your dripping cunt with an open mouth and bared teeth. I ravage your delicate cunt meat as you lay back on the counter. You moan loudly and then scream as you cum hard into my sucking mouth; I enjoy my lunch.

CHAPTER 23

No Hurry

I lower you gently on the bed and reach for your pants. As I pull them gently down your legs, I back away so I can slide them free of you. I reach up and hook as I get them down to your ankles and off; reach up, hook my fingers gently in your panty band on both sides so I can ease your panties down the same way. Slowly, steadily, I move them down to your ankles before I yank them off and toss them onto the chair.

I glance up at you; you look down at me, your head on the pillow.

"First things first."

You smile to yourself as you hear the huskiness already in my voice and see the lustful glint in my eyes. You shiver a little with pleasure at the touch of my hands on your legs. As you watch me spread your legs, you close your eyes and breathe out. You feel me bring your knees up, and you let out a quiet surprised gasp. As I turn you onto your stomach, you feel my hands lift your hips, followed by the first long lap of my tongue on your pussy. Your stomach tightens, and you bite your lip as the lapping starts in earnest; it's enough to inspire you to arch your back down and push back slightly.

"That tongue feels wonderful, doesn't it?" I ask.

In response, you shudder again as you push back and feel my tongue ease in.

"Ohhh God yeah," you moan.

"You do enjoy a talented and devoted pussy-eater, don't you?" I say passionately.

You groan into the pillow as my tongue teases your clit hood. I plunge deeper, and now your clit is under my skillful tongue. Your labia swells, and your juices form as my tongue manipulates your hardening clit just the way you need it. My mouth lips on your pussy lips, my nose brushing on the nether skin and on your asshole. Your rational thoughts fade as your mind and body relax into sex mode.

My tongue tip flickers up and down your juicy slit. My mouth, warm and wet, opens wide and presses down on your horny mound, my tongue dabbing at your thrumming, erect clit. You groan softly into the pillow again and stretch out luxuriously and sensually. As you feel my hands move under you, your breathing grows deep and slow; you exhale as you feel me feel your hardening—fuck it, your *hard*—nipples. You gasp at the sudden, deliciously cool-then-hot sting of the tight, tight pinch followed by shock of electricity within. The lightning strikes in your pussy, and you press your face down toward your breasts, the pleasure so intense you curl up slightly. Seconds later, your core decides it's time; you lift your head with intent, force yourself back on the edges of pleasure rapidly knifing through your body, and press back with your entire body.

You feel your pussy fill with my busy mouth and tongue and lips. You squeal quietly to yourself as you feel my hands on your thighs, and then you whimper in frustration as you realize I am in no hurry. The hard tongue firmly fucks your cunt; the tongue tip bullies your tingling clit with a surgeon's precise touch, and I pull your swollen labia into my mouth.

As I service you, it is drawn and massaged and released and squeezed by the movements of my jaw and mouth. I press my firm nose on the sensitive, puckered skin of your asshole. You remember my shy face as it begs you to let me; it touches you as much as it turns you on, and the need for cock grows within as you keep your knees back for me.

You fall to your side and feel my hands slide easily around. I shift you onto your back and push your knees to your chest.

"Ohh, God," you whisper desperately, "there's the … to the … ohh fuck right there … yes, right there, baby."

My tongue, wide and soft and firm as a hand now, fills your cunt just the way you like it. Your hands come down and find the hair on my head; you groan out loud, and I feel your cunt grip down hard on my tongue. You are so beautiful. It's the four of us now—you, me, your cunt, and my tongue. It's pussy-fuck time, tongue style, and you are loving it. You grip my hair and lift your body slightly as you stomach muscles tighten and you scream.

"Fuck me, fuck me … fuck!"

You are going to cum, I observe with satisfaction. Your hands are tight in my hair as your face tightens and contorts and then goes slack. Your mouth opens, and the barest of whispering whimpers emerge as your body is wracked violently by a tremendous orgasm that sparks white-hot in every cell and every part of your body. The second one pounds through the first, and your cunt explodes, just as it was designed to do. You feel the gush of juice and my tongue going strong.

"Oh, oh, honey …" you whimper. "Ohhh sweetie, yes, the clit, ohh-my-Godddd!"

My finger slides into your perfect ass, and the combination sends you into a silent-scream orgasm that stops your breath and tightens every muscle in your body.

Chapter 24

Edged

Cradled in my arm yet still bound, the leather belt warm and giving, you reach for glass I offer with your lips. You are blindfolded yet aware of the dark and the warmth of the room; the cold of the wine on your tongue is a pleasing contrast for your senses. You feel womanly and feminine and helpless and babied, reduced and enabled and encouraged. The second sip of wine washes over your tongue and the back of your throat; you swallow gratefully. The feel of another orgasm swells again in your gut as your pussy warms with the dull ache of cock-need. You hear me place the wine glass on the nightstand, and in the next moment, you feel my fingers work the silk knot behind your head. As the ends come apart, you see the blindfold fall away, and you can see again. You turn your head up to look at me, but I have turned away. You hear the drawer open and close; I turn back, holding something in my hand. It's compact and mechanical; it looks like it may be made of chrome. Your hands move by themselves again, and you realize you must have dropped the chain. You make a mental note of that fact as you stare at the object turning in my hand. I can see that you are about to risk it all and ask me what it is. Before you can speak, I bring it down to your breast. You stare down as best you can, and you see the hole of the metal object lowered onto your nipple. I press the object on the top of your nipple, encapsulating it. You feel the edge of the metal ring on the areola base, and then you feel the squeezing sensation. Your eyes widen; you can't look away. You can't speak or form words as the fingers continue to tighten the device. The pressure becomes fire, and you see that the tip of your nipple is now dark red. The metal clamps grows tighter and tighter; the pain radiates up and out like wildfire—and it does not stop. I turn away from you for a moment, but I don't think you know it.

Your breath erupts from you, once held but no longer. You watch as the fingers continue their unhurried turning of the device. Your nipple is on fire, trapped within the shiny steel. Your breast becomes something strange and alien, yet real as you experience a pain you have imagined.

I turn back to you, and I see the surprise in your eyes. You look at my other hand, and you see the other clamp. I head directly to your other nipple; you have to look, don't you? You *have* to feel your other precious nipple as I assault it. I stuff your nipple into the metal and drive it down to the base of your nubbin; only a tiny sliver of the tiny, pink tip of your nipple remains visible. There is no discussion, no pause. The fingers find the screw and turn it. You feel the squeeze again as I tighten the clamp without pause or even mercy. Soon, you feel the same sting, the same cold-burning but white-hot pain. In a matter of only a few moments, the tip of your nipple turns an angry, frightened, dark shade of red.

You look down at the clamps and look up at me, your eyes soft and questioning. I can see that you are both half-smiling and not smiling at all; the pain bites and stings.

Your nipples are now distended orbs of pain and pleasure. You look up at me, excited and a little panicked. I am on one elbow as I stare, calm and lustful and detached, into your eyes. Without breaking my gaze, I lift my hand. You watch me, uncertain; then you feel my hand go around your thigh. I turn my hand palm-up and begin to graze my limp fingers down the wet mat of your spasming, hungry pussy. The backs of my fingernails slide down over the damp hair to the bottom; I barely touch on the dripping hole of your cunt before I pull away. I go back up to the top to caress you slowly. I can be patient. I slide my fingers back down to the bottom, unhurried. I look down at you as you look up at me with hopeful eyes and a hesitant, game smile. Your body rewards me with tiny jerking movements as it tightens then relaxes and bucks without your input. Your pussy responds to the fingers as they graze, slowly and repetitively. I touch you randomly and sadistically on your desperately hard clit, sending spikes of raw voltage through your curled and helpless body.

You are breathing even harder now, your nipples numb in the cold fire. Your body stays tight as you feel my hand stop and settle on your mound, my fingers tormenting you with a series of back-and-forth plunges on your clit. Your wrists pull on the belt, and you feel yourself going under; the level of stimulation is now too intense to bear, and the *need* to cum takes over. You try to resist, but you can't help it.

"Oh God," you plead. "Please—"

You turn your head on the pillow and look up into my eyes with pushed-to-the-edge total sincerity.

"Oh God … I need to cum. Please, baby, let me …"

You see the hand come around your thigh and up toward you. The next thing you know, your head is turned from the force of the slap. Your lips touch on the pillow before you look back. The left side of your face is on fire now, and your ears ring. Your chin is pinched suddenly, and you feel pain from my fingers and the angle of your head.

"I will cum you when *I* am ready, is that clear?"

For a moment, you hold your body and face perfectly still in the grip. My eyes are hard and cold now, and you are crushed by my tone. To your sexually stressed mind, this is a threat. Your rational mind takes a back seat to your submission; you try to nod, even as your pussy swells with an intense orgasm that is about to pop, about to explode. You can only blink up into those fierce and burning eyes.

The hand is gone as quickly as it appeared before it slapped your face. It goes back down and around your thigh. You moan, but it gets trapped in your throat as you feel your clit suddenly and viciously fingered. The fingering is a clear attempt to draw out the huge about-to-happen orgasm nestled in your cunt. There's no turning back, no holding back now as your cunt folds up and explodes. A tidal wave of pleasure races out of you, past the thrumming, bloated, red coal of your screaming clit.

"No no … no arghhhhhunhhhh … oooh fuck!"

You sob and scream out as the well head deep, deep in your pussy blows wide open. The orgasm is huge, too rapid, and you are deaf, dumb and blind—and awestruck in this final moment. Some part of you feels the fingering stop, but all of you feels the first slam of flat man hand on your cunt and you lose it totally. The hard slap on your cunt as it oozes and creams takes you over the edge and into space. You cum and cum; there is nothing else but a long-denied pleasure that comes full-on and generous and unstopping from your soul.

You hear yourself breathe. You open your eyes and glance down between your thighs and calves to look at the belt. You feel the belt on your wrists again, and it all comes back to you. You realize you were sleeping just now. You squint your eyes and blink a couple of times before you turn your head toward me. I am there, and in my eyes, you see a look of calm adoration and patience. I hold up a bottle of spring water and bring it to your lips. I allow you to drink deeply before I ease the bottle away and place it on the nightstand. I return with a tray of sliced fruit. You glance down at the tray, at me, and then back down at the tray. I lift a melon slice from the tray and touch it to your lips. You open your mouth and take in the melon, your lips around the toothpick as I slide it gently out and place it on the tray. The melon juices and melts in your mouth, and you feel secure, you feel loved, you feel cared for and calm in my protective arms. You are relaxed; as you wake up and come back to the world, you look up into my eyes and smile. The offered strawberry is ripe and delicious and squishy in your mouth, as are the wisping vagaries in your stomach and pussy. You glance up at me, ready to go, your eyes smoky and sparkling with a silent request for more that you can barely hold back.

The tray still in my hands, I lean down and bring my face close to yours and pause. Our eyes meet, and the silent words of love and trust and knowing pass and flow between us. You feel my breath first, warm and soft, and then my barely-there lips on yours. It is a moment of naked openness and passion. I look into your eyes again as I move away slowly to the edge of the bed. Your eyes locked in mine as I stand, my hands go to the front of my jeans, and my fingers slowly lower the zipper to expose the V-opening and the fringe of pubic hair. I lower my jeans, the first curve exposed to you. I straighten up, and see you stare at my cock, thick and half-hard and ready. You look down at the wide purplish-pink head and the dark slit, the ridge edge and the shaft, the blue-green of the vein going back, and I can see your body tingling. Your breath grows shallow, and I can sense the despair you feel; the distance between your bound self and this cock is intolerable. Your wrists move in the belt, and your stomach flutters as the intention becomes clear; it's you and that cock. You swallow hard, and I come closer to the edge of the bed. I grab you, pull you, turn you. You feel your upper body being guided toward the edge of the bed; your stomach and pussy tense-tight and quivering, your tongue on your lips, your eyes and face serious and expectant, I slide you along the sheets and position you as I choose. My hands, strong and sure on your shoulders, you feel the edge of the mattress under the base of your skull. Your head is pulled slightly over the edge, and you stare up at the ceiling helplessly. There is no way to hang on or steady yourself or save yourself. You glance up and try to catch my eye, but I am not looking at you. My arms are on your shoulders, and you can *almost* see the cock directly behind your head but you can't—until you are pulled a little closer to the edge. Your head tilts back—and there it is.

It's harder now. It points upward now, and you can see the base of the shaft and the ridge line going up, the black hairs, and the wrinkled skin of the ball sack. I lean forward for a moment, and you look from the muscled ridges of my stomach to the bottom of my chest. You are down, down here, down below the muscled chest and stomach, alone and intimate with a thick cock so close you could kiss it—and you want to. That's what you do; you suck cock, hard cock; you take hard cock down your throat, and yes, you would beg for a throat-fuck and you just might. Your pussy spasms and clenches, and you nose-suck the scent and smell of fresh hard cock deep into your lungs as you stare up, quiet and ready.

I tilt your head back so your neck is supported by the edge of the bed. You look up at your man's cock and the bottom of his ball sack, both balls lifted, tight, and firm. You can see the base of the cock and little else; it's straight up now, a thick, primal spear. You stare up intently at me, utterly focused the upper part and two-heart head of the cock. The cock bobs down, lifts itself; you touch your tongue to your lips, very aware of your throat and your role. You feel my hands graze lightly along your shins and touch on your knees. The light in the room is low and warm. As I straighten up, our eyes meet; you see me look at your legs and body with hunger. I look down at you, my face and eyes simultaneously far above but very close. You see tension in my face, as well as in my balls and cock. I'm just above your face, my need for *this* and for *you* equal in my eyes. Suddenly and clearly, you understand how much you are a part of and responsible for this; the engorged cock, steel hard and bobbing from sexual tension, is just above your face. You think of our late-night make-out sessions out on the couch, where we shared whispered desires, including your love of throat-fucking. I think back to how turned on I was to hear you speak of how much I turn you on, but you knew that from the way this cock moved under your hand. Your mind-pussy jumps again at the thought of it.

You feel and see my hands press gently on the sides of your head; there's nothing you can do now, and there's no place you'd rather be. My cock, balls, and base move back into view, the shaft above you. It moves directly over your eyes and stops. My hands grab your head, and with great care and controlled restraint, I lower the ball sack and cock so it brushes your forehead and hair. I then brush it down your forehead and nose before I rest the shaft and balls on your face. We both emit a low, breathy groan of pleasure.

My masculine hands grip your head as you breathe slowly, deliciously aware of the weight of my penis on your forehead, nose, and chin. My hairs of my ball sack tickle your eyes and almost blind you. In the intimate quarters below your man's cock, you are aware of the darkness as well as my warmth and scent. You feel the muscled weight and heft of my engorged cock as it slides forward and back along the center of your face. An excited, primal, biological necessity overtakes you, centered on the impending release from my sperm-laden balls and the erotic pleasure of me inseminating your throat.

You encouraged this; you hinted at this; you let me know this was possible, and my face is polite and questioning and concerned for your safety. My eyes hold a sudden, fiery passion at the same time, and you saw that immediately. Barely aware of my words, you nod calmly to assure me that this it was okay, that this is what you want. Your pussy is knotted tight with desire; it *demands* to orgasm. Your hard nub of a clit throbs as you stare into my eyes. They speak volumes to me: you *want* what you saw there. You *want* the cock abuse; you *want* to be dominated. You see the promise of it all in my cool, glittery, predatory stare. You squirm and press your sopping pussy onto the couch pillows. You smile and nod, and I can see how proud you are of how well you have manipulated your dom to give you just what *you* desire this time. I smile, proud of how well you have used your many gifts to instruct me in your pleasure. Your glances are all the confession of desire I need; encouraged and excited, the cock-master sadist will come out and take you.

The middle of your face is all cock now; your mouth is warm, wet, and slack, your tongue up. It slides forward and back on my warm rod; it moves and readies itself. As you look up and see the predator in my eyes, your gut drops and flutters. *Hello, Mister Cock Sadist,* your eyes say to me. *I've been craving you.* Suddenly, the first tingle of another deep orgasm wells up inside you. You want this, and you want this *right. Fucking. Now.* Ever the dutiful submissive, you hunger to be put in your place by hard cock. Quickly and without warning, I slip I my hard cock through your waiting lips.

"Suck, bitch!" I command. "Suck, you bitch. Suck, you cock-whore."

"Of course, yes … of course, sir," you mumble around my manhood in your mouth.

Be a big girl, you think, as the cock slides back and stops. You feel the angle change, and then your mouth is packed with cock again. Your lips close lightly around the head. I give you a mouthful, a fuck-mouthful, and your eyes close. Your cheeks touch on the sides as your tongue explores me. Your mouth feels rounded and full, and you moan a muffled whimper of pure animal pleasure as you feel me move inside you. The sudden dull thud of a baseball at the back of your throat startles you briefly, but then you accept it. I press hard for a moment and then relax. I'm too big, way too big to go further, but I press hard again and feel your throat round and stretch in an attempt to accommodate me. Your hands are flat on the bed, as your whole, sweaty, sexy body tightens as it strains to accept all of me.

Your lips around the shaft and your throat work as a team as I wedge my rod deep within you with increasing force and intent. Your pulse pounds in your ears; you are totally focused on the task at hand. Your pussy spasms violently, and you lift your hands up and bring them back to grab my thighs. You pull me closer, desperate and crazed for cock. You hear me groan out loud, and your mind stops as you feel the sudden, piercing press of man muscle; your throat giving way to the searing pleasure-pain as it stretches to unnatural proportions. It's mind blowing; no words can describe the primal feel of my cock as it slides in and down. In a single, lunging thrust, I own your throat.

My fingertips brush your stomach; I feel your hands leave the backs of my thighs. Your arms and hands drop slowly down to the mattress. I look down, my chest and stomach pressed to your neck and chin, your lower lip curved back around the hint of cock shaft and my pubic hair. Your throat is pronounced; it looks strained. I hold myself in position as a series of stuttering gasps and low, tortured groans of pleasure escape as I feel my hips buck. As I send my cock deeper, my pubic hairs touch your face. I groan loudly through gritted teeth and force myself to pull back, to pull it back. My hips go back, and I ease my cock slowly out. I grimace at the pleasure of your throat as it grips my cock tightly. I feel this on every inch of me. Every inch screams with pleasure and desire and gratitude. Ohhh fuck, this feels good. The tightness of your throat and the wet space of your mouth are paradise. As I arch my back and lift my cock the last few inches out of your mouth, you choke and a bit of spittle flies from your lips. You gasp and try to recover. With your hands on my sides, I look down and lower my hips again. My cock head enters your slackened mouth and hits the back of your throat as my hips follow through with a muscled shove. My dick is fully in your throat again, balls deep. Your hands open and close, and you whimper as I lift my hips and lower them, sizing up your throat for the fucking to come.

My body is muscled, tight, and poised. I look down at your sweaty, sexy breasts and see your hard nipples. You move your legs and moan; it's obvious that you enjoy my cock in your throat. As my balls tighten at your erotic sexiness, my jaw tightens. My eyes go calm and steady as I lift with my hips and raise my cock up. Enrobed in the tight, gripping slide of your throat, the pleasure is too intense. The crown of the head of my cock passes through the tight ring of the back of your throat ; I groan out loud and let the weight of my hips spear my cock back in deep. I slide in and out of the back of your throat, and it's all I can do not to cum, not to give in to the intense urge to empty my balls, to cum hard and coat your throat—but I hold off. The glove of your throat stroking my cock and your satisfied purrs and mewlings are agony for me. My pubic hair touches lightly on your nose and cheeks, and I can only hold on for a moment; I have to draw back. My ass cheeks dimple, and my calves cry out in sharp relief as I feel my cock head pop clear of your throat. I feel your tongue as you lick and worship me, and I look up at the ceiling and breathe. Shaky and filled with adoration and amazement, I touch your shoulders lightly before my hips plunge forward to force feed my throbbing cock back into your clutching throat.

"Ohhhh Godddd …"

The head of my cock is down somewhere very deep in your throat, and I feel my balls touch and settle relaxed on your eyes and cheekbones. You moan a long, low moan of pleasure, your knees up and your feet flat on the bed. Slowly, sensually, and indulgently, you arrange your long, gorgeous legs to one side. You then slowly lift and lay them over to the other side. As you suck me, I can see how much you enjoy pleasuring yourself on my throbbing club of a cock. I have never been this hard—this *painfully* hard—or this pleasured in my life. I use everything I have to keep my cock at your disposal. I slowly move it up and down as you devour and play with me. I look up at the ceiling and bite my lip so hard I draw blood, but the pleasure is unprecedented. I ride your throat lustfully and then dutifully and then back again, the fine line of our roles blurred in the raw heat of the sexual and sensual experience between us. Your knees are up, and I lean forward suddenly. I part them down to your pussy, and in flash, my face is there. I lick and suck on your juices as I work my cock, slowly and lovingly in your attentive mouth.

I slide my hands down and grip your ass cheeks as I lick down your slit. I press my open mouth on your mound and suck. I take in your juices and slather my tongue wildly, without technique or thought. Your labia are on my cheeks and I shovel-drive my hard tongue down your slit repeatedly until I can't take it anymore. As I pull you in by your ass cheeks and sink my tongue into the pink-skinned wetness of your spasming, sexy cunt, you moan deeply around my peaking bone-hard cock. My mind goes blank, and my head bobs, my neck muscles strained. I tongue-fuck your juicy pussy with an intensity and desperation that arches you back and lifts your hips. You press your cunt up into my tongue and mouth, and it's all happening—and it's all too much. I close my eyes and slam-lock my cock; I feel my balls catch and pull into your mouth. I'm so deep, and my balls lift and tighten painfully.

"Oohhhh-mother-fucker-oohh-God." A gurgle, incoherently.

Your pussy is wide open for me. It grips and squirts on my tongue and in my mouth. As you scream out, your thick, delicious pussy juice fills my mouth, and now I'm cumming hard. Your mouth closes around my pumping balls, and your moaning sends me over the edge.

"Ohhhh God!" I scream as I cum hard in your throat. You swallow your juices eagerly. You cum a second and then a third time as I throat-fuck you more. Moaning, we both collapse. I am done; I have to stop. I pull out and fall back on the bed, my head near your thighs.

I sit up, fighting for breath. I look down at you; you turn your head toward me and look into my eyes. Your face is calm and serious before you smile up at me but also satisfied and knowing. I hunch forward to the edge of the bed and stand up to walk to the master bath. You hear me turn on the shower, and a moment later, I reappear. I walk back over to the bed and gently ease you into my arms. We are serious and smiling, lustful and affectionate. I bring my face down close to yours and graze my lips to yours. I can't hold back anymore; I kiss you deeply. My hands go around your shoulders, and our kiss consumes us, our sex in the distant past.

In this moment, this kiss is all we are and all we want to be.

My lips lift up away from yours. As I stare into your eyes, my eyes soften and twinkle. Quickly, softly, gently, I kiss you before I turn and stand. I offer you my hand and invite you to join me in the shower. Like our love, it runs full-on, hot, and steaming.

CHAPTER 25

Holiday

The morning passes in a flurry of chores and holiday preparations around the house. You clean everything, and when the house is spotless, you move on to the decorations. The wreath on the door, the scented candles, the pine tree, are all your little touches to make the house a home for the holidays. You love the dining table in particular, dressed up with sleigh placemats and centerpiece of a wreath and candles. You hear the car pull in; you glance at the clock. It's a little past 11:00 a.m. As you come into the kitchen, you see me coming in the back door.

"Hey!"

"Hey! Hi, you!"

In my arms, I have a bag. I place it casually on the kitchen table so I can take you in my arms instead. I kiss you softly on the lips.

"Well, this is nice! Did you come home for lunch? We have some leftover stew I could heat up."

I look at you with the sparkling eyes and calm intensity of a dom, your dom. You feel your pussy twinge and your stomach flutter; your words trail off as you match my stare and wait.

"I didn't come home for lunch."

"No?"

"No."

"Oh," you say with hope in your voice. "I see."

I kiss you again, this time slowly and deeply. As you feel my hands move to the front of your blouse, you kiss back. You feel the tug on your shirt; I pull it out from your jeans, my hands going under and up to your bra. My fingers go under the edges of the cups, up and on top of your breasts. My tongue, sudden and insistent, enters your mouth as my fingers find your hardening nipples. You gasp into my mouth as I pinch your nipples tightly and begin to roll them slowly back and forth.

My hands go down on your hips as your hands reach up to touch my arms. We stare into each other's eyes, the sexual heat rising between us unchecked. In the quiet of the house, the everyday giving way to the magic we have between us, the vanilla world fades as our hunger for each other rises. Our eyes remain locked, and you feel my hands tighten on your hips. I urge you backward, your hands on my forearms. I can tell that you are about to say something, to ask a question, but once you feel the edge of the table on your ass, that goes away. I don't stop; I lean you back and hoist you up on the edge of the dining-room table. I move your lovely centerpiece over and ease you down on the table, your bent legs over the edge. You are surprised and curious and about to speak, but I have already turned away. I go to the kitchen table and pick up the bag.

I come back and stand between your legs for a moment. I place the bag down by your thigh; you feel *something* in the bag. My hands move to the front of your jeans; my fingers find and undo the stud and then find the zipper tab and pull your zipper down. Your jeans open, I tug your jeans down, past the curve of your ass, down midthigh, down to your ankles, and off. You are in your panties and blouse on your dining-room table. Your man doesn't look up. He doesn't smile at you. You feel hands at your panties, so you lift your hips and feel your panties passing under you. In a flash, they are gone. With your legs over the side and the warm room air on your exposed bush, your pulse races. *This is so unfamiliar,* you think. *It's not something we do on the dining-room table.* You want to say that, but you don't. You want this to stop, but your pussy throbs and aches for me. You don't really want this to stop at all. *Keep going,* you beg me silently. *Please keep going.*

You watch me reach down, and you feel my hands on your ankle. I raise your leg and bend your knee back toward your breast. My hand on your shin, I reach into the bag with my other hand to pull out a length of white—rope, braided white rope. I grab your wrist and lay your forearm against your shin and loop the rope over at your elbow and knee. I come around to face your arm and shin, and I begin to wrap the rope snugly tight around your shin and forearm. I wrap the thick, silken rope in neat, efficient rows down toward your wrist and ankle.

Your hair touches the wreath centerpiece, and you feel the polished mahogany wood hard under your back. With your right hand and arm lying by your side, you watch wide-eyed, your breath coming in short gasps as you watch me work. You watch as I bind your left forearm to your shin and wrap it in neat rows. Your forearm flat and tight to your shin, I tie off both your wrist and ankle. You watch me run my fingertips down the rows, back up to your elbow and knee, as I check for tightness. You feel it inside — the throbbing, burning, tingling overexcitement of a craving that is about to finally be addressed. You watch me bring my face down close to the rope rows, where I place a soft, tender kiss before I move away. Your knee remains close to your breast and your forearm stays tight on your shin; nothing is going anywhere. I am over at your other side now and you relax. You try to move your left arm, but it is part of a unit now; your left arm and left leg move as one. A shimmery wave of coital tremors ripples through your body. Your eyes half-close as a hazy sex-heat fills your mind, and you are drifting down, down into your submission. You are a submissive, in mind and soul, and your pussy is a twinging, wet mess.

You turn your head to me, and you watch and feel me grab your wrist and lift your arm. Your eyes take it all in: my calm, intense face and efficient hands; your forearm aligned and bound to your shin; the white rope going over both, around and over and around again. You don't move your arm or your leg at all, and you wouldn't for the world. You are cooperating in your bondage, holding yourself still. Even as you try to handle the tightening and coiling and relaxing of your pre-orgasmic body, you bite on your lower lip and breathe hard. My face goes down close, and you feel the gentle bump of a tender kiss through the rope. I step away, and you realize you have time by yourself, with your bondage. You pull with a sudden, hard effort on your arms and legs all at the same time; you go nowhere, but you do rock once—barely. Your vulnerability is a real and hard fact; your pussy feels wide open and exposed, your breasts are on fire, your nipples are rock-hard and brushing under your blouse. Your heart is racing, your pulse a drum in your temples. You breathe out hard and whimper like a little girl; with a mixture of awe and fright, you almost fear the huge orgasms building, brand new and deep, in your aching pussy.

When I turn back toward you and stand between your spread and bound legs, you stare wide-eyed at me. I look back at you with a serious intensity. You notice that I am staring at your chest, clearly thinking about something as I reach up with slow, intention-driven hands, and open your blouse. As I open each button with a careful efficiency, my fingertips press on your sensitive chest. My hands move down your front, to your stomach, and then come back up. I open your blouse in neat halves and lay them on your bra-covered breasts. You are barely breathing, but you still feel the push and pinch of my fingers on the clasp, and then your bra is open. You feel my fingers again at the bottom wires of the cups, and soon, the cups are lifted off. The sensation of the room air on your naked breasts causes your nipples to pulse to a new hardness. Everything is sexual now; your mind races, your pussy pulses, punkish. Now that your breasts are exposed to the room, you need hard cock even more now.

I straighten up and pause and look down at you with eyes far removed from lovemaking, from the both of us under the covers giggling. You try to read the cold, white-hot glint in the eyes of the man you *thought* you knew, the man who—barely an hour ago—you thought had come home for lunch. Who is this man, the one who seduced you as he always could, the man who has you trussed and naked on your dining-room table? The dark thoughts and desires burn between you now.

My arm moves up and past your head and returns just as quickly; you see one of the candles from the centerpiece in my hand. It's one of the brand-new candles you bought just yesterday. My hand pauses deliberately over your breasts, and my other hand comes into view. In it I hold a lighter. First, you hear the gritty sound of the lighter being put to use. Then you see the yellow-and-blue flame. You see every detail, every one—the flame, the lighter, the candle, the hand. You see the flame touch on the white virgin wick, and you think back to the day before. You bought those candles yourself; you bought those candles yesterday. *They were so nice, so perfect for the table wreath,* you think. You watch as I light the wick, discard the lighter, and allow the flame to grow. You watch the wax warm up as the hand brings the candle closer to your breast. You feel the flame and the heat as your nipple grows an angry pink at the top; it's very near the flame, you realize. Your body pulls suddenly, but you don't move at all. You feel the heat now for real; you see the wax melting. You tense again and buck in the ropes as your stomach flip-flops. As you watch the first drop forming and the drop of hot wax fall, your heart races as the first hard orgasm thumps in your pussy.

The drop of wax lands on the tip of your nipple, pinprick painful. The pain-pleasure radiates, leaving you tense. You can do nothing but stare. As a second drop falls and then a third, you are wide-eyed. A rising orgasm looms, and you are left fidgety and focused on the flame. You feel and fear the pain from each new drop of wax; you both fear and love the hand that turns and tends the candle. As the flame grows bigger, the flow of wax becomes steadier. Your nipple is red hot, a glowing coal of passion and pain. Your nipple has started to wax over, and it feels so good, so rich, so fucking awesome. You can feel more orgasms form in your dripping cunt. The wax, cool and hard, pinches on your burned and swollen nipple. Your eyes follow the hand and the candle and the flame as it moves slowly over to your other nipple, which remains untouched and fresh and tender—and throbbing and rock hard. The hand holds the flame directly over you. You see the same pinkish-red of nipple in the glow as the candle is tilted. The hot wax drips down on you. With each new drip, you feel the same searing heat; the pain-pleasure rolls through you again as your nipple disappears under the wax.

With each breath, you sigh with relief and pleasure. You look down at the warm wax that has formed a hard shell on each of your nipples. You glance at your arms extended on both sides, and you take in the rows of white rope. You are in a canyon formed of your own legs and arms, and the white, tight rope that is keeping you like this. It keeps you on your back and exposed. You glance down past your stomach to your bush and then to the kitchen beyond that. You see the refrigerator and the notes and papers on the refrigerator door, and you are reminded of how much life has just changed. Now you are on your dining-room table, naked and bound, a total cock- and pain-slut for everyone and anyone to see. At the thought, your pussy goes huge and juicy; it's puffy and tingling, electric and bloated, with impatient orgasms waiting to be birthed. They demand to happen, but there is nothing you can do. You lose sight of both the candle and my hand for a moment. When it returns to your view, the hand is now holding the centerpiece. I remove another virgin candle from the centerpiece. You glance at me, and of course, I'm not looking at you. I'm looking at the candle, and the look in my eyes scares you. That look alone is enough to push you over the edge, so you look back at the candle. The hand flips the candle and displays the base, the bottom of the candle to you. You look at the details that keep the candle in the holder, the grooves and ridges, and you wince.

The hand moves suddenly and goes down, down to your pussy. *Ooh God, oh God*, you think. *In my pussy? Oh God.* You feel the swipe, the hard swipe as I drag the candle base down your wet wet slit, and you almost cum. The sensation is so sudden and intense and real, your pussy goes to white fire. You feel the candle butt touch hard on your clit hood and then it's dragged down your slit again. Barely a moment later, you feel the big wheels begin to turn deep within you. They begin to turn the mountains and everything shifts around in your cunt. The candle plows down again, rude and rough. *Oh yeah, you are going to cum,* you think. *You are going to cum …here it comes, here it comes … oh my God!*

You look up at me, eyes and mouth open, unbelieving. The candle is in your ass, and it's sliding deeper. As you feel it going deeper in your ass, a jittery-queasy feeling rolls over your whole body. Your asshole tightens its grip and slides on wax. The candle fullness feels like it touches just below your stomach before the sensation eases. You glance down, horrified and giddy, shocked and turned on, at the sight of the candle poking out from your ass. The candle feels so good as it slides in and out of your ass. You love the sensation of being ass-fucked by this candle. You love anal sex, and this is all weird and wonderful and new. You are being ass-fucked, you fuck-slut, you slut-whore, and you can't help but cry out in pleasure.

"Ohh …fuck, fuck, fuck me … feels so good … don't stop, please don't, please don't—"

You coil hard in the ropes with all of your strength, every muscle and emotion and thought consuming you as the first orgasm forms up hard and huge and explodes inside your spasming pussy. You feel it in your whole body, in your stomach, in your arms and legs, in your fingertips and eyelids. The sploogey gush of pussy juice exhausts you, and you stare, immobilized, paralyzed, unable to do anything but orgasm again. As the candle smooth-pistons in your ass, you cum again, and then a third fourth and fifth time. At the sixth, you scream out like you never have before; you have never cum like this before. You can't feel or think of anything else as your body wracks violently in the unyielding ropes.

There is no retreat, no place to hide; you grit your teeth and close your eyes. Your modesty and your upbringing find you for a moment, and you groan with deep embarrassment. You feel the heat on your face as you are reminded of the candle in your ass. *I have a candle … in my ass,* you think. Then you feel it slide out, the smooth wax a torture on the inside of your puckering hole. You feel the ridged base, and then you feel it turn inside you. Back and forth, back and forth, you glance down and you see the rest of the candle between my palm. I roll the candle back and forth, so the base ridges rotate back and forth inside of you. You can't take it; the pervy-dirtiness of it all. You cum—hard. You shudder in your bondage and cum with a candle rotating in your butt. It feels so good, so filthy, so pleasurable, and so incredible, you cry out and cry out again, gasping and weepy.

I ease the candle out of your ass. You half-open your eyes, and you see me step back. Slowly and deliberately, I open my belt, undo the clasp of my slacks, and lower them. I then push my brief down to midthigh and straighten up. Your eyes grow wide as you take in the sight of my cock, harder and bigger than you have ever seen it before. This is so different from the gentle, make-love, tender cock you know that a chill goes through you; a delicious chill rises and throbs up and crests tingling on your pussy lips. Your tongue touches on your dry lips as you look up at my intense eyes and then back down at the bobbing club of cock. The wide apple head, angry, red, and huge, is aimed directly at your delicate, unprotected pussy.

Your body tight, tingling, and on fire with anticipation, you stare down from between your bound arms and legs; you know what is about to happen. You also know it will be different. You feel the intensity in your own eyes. Bound and helpless and aroused to a level you have only dreamed about, thought about, you feel something only hinted at by your own body during your most intense vanilla orgasms, when you screamed out and hugged close and came. You were all there, but there was still a part of you, a background part of you that wasn't touched, wasn't breached, wasn't taken. There remained a back-of-your-mind private part of your mind that was never offered or touched. You sense that that is all about to change.

You watch me bring my hand to my cock and touch it. Without looking at you, I move forward and place the head, carefully and perfectly, at your cunt. You feel the spongy wideness and your gut tightens; you hear me breathe out with my own tension as my hands tighten painfully. My hands are forgotten as you feel the sudden spearing fullness of hard cock. As my body pushes in and fills the area between your bound thighs, my arms come up. I pull you roughly to me and go immediately into a muscled cocking of your dripping cunt that stops your breath. Your orgasm blooms up from the deepest part of you, and there is nothing else but this orgasm and the cock turning your spasming pussy to a thrumming, tingling, greedy mush. You tense up and go limp in your ropes, and you cum hard. You begin to gush, your body and soul open to the pleasure. Your shaking body contracts into the orgasm that immediately follows; you press and strain on the ropes as your orgasm comes from everywhere at once, hot and wonderfully intense. Your eyes tear up and your hands clutch the ropes, and there is more cock, more hard cock.

Safe in the warm, reddish haze of your overstimulated mind, your deepest cravings met, you reflect. These orgasms have left you spent in the way sex was meant to; there are no words in your mind, only an intuitive sense of being newly aware. You open your eyes enough to see and take in the ropes and the hands and this man between your legs. He is so much your man and much more: he is your master. You stare, calm and sure and at peace, his cock deep inside you, and his eyes down on your body. The look in his eyes is thoughtful and preoccupied and intense.

You gasp quietly as I pull out abruptly and turn away from you. I walk into the kitchen and return a moment later, holding something. It's your clothespin bag. I am between your legs again, and I drop the bag casually on the table near your side. You feel your heart race again as you stare at my hand. I reach into the bag, and my hand comes out with one of the clothespins. I squeeze it and then let it snap shut, all for your benefit. *Oh God,* you think, *the spring, the spring in those things!* You watch as I bring a clothespin to wax-covered nipple, and open it wide. I push it down on your nipple, and the wax crushes under the force. With my other hand, I grip your breast to force it straight up. The jaws of the clothespin wedges onto your nipple, and you gasp at the sudden heat and sting of it. When both hands move away, only the clothespin remains, tight and painful and wooden and half laying on your breast. You feel your other breast as I pull it up and grip it, and you turn your head to observe as I clip another clothespin on your other nipple. Your breath shallow and quick, you feel that both of your nipples on fire.

"How do they feel."

This is spoken, not asked; you look up into my eyes, and in that moment, we are strangers who have just met.

"Good … sir."

In an instant, your whispered reply makes us soul mates. We are as we truthfully are, your submissive to my dominant, your slave to my master.

Our eyes locked, I reach down and pull the candle in one tug smoothly from your ass; you hear it drop onto the floor.

"I'm going to have your ass."

You nod, another whisper. "Yes."

I bring my hand up and touch lightly on the clothespins, first one then the other. I lift them up and let them drop with a casual toss, causing fresh pain to tingle from your nipples.

"Because you are my slave."

"Yes."

"My slut."

"Yes."

"My cock-slut … who needs her ass fucked."

"Yes … yes, sir."

Our eyes are locked, and our conversation is quiet and measured and intense; so much has been revealed, yet so much changes moment by moment, word by word. My hand moves down over your stomach and over the edge. I can feel your tight stomach; every movement is registered. You take in every detail—the opened, unbuttoned front of my white-collared shirt; my chest and stomach underneath and my pubic hair; the scent of your pussy; the scent of my cologne; the wood on your swollen breasts . You sense the sudden up-and-down motion and firm probing push of my cock head on your asshole. You reveal the quick heat of embarrassment on your face; your face is tense and wanting. I look down and feel the increasing pressure down there, the sting. I straighten up, lean forward, and look at you again. You look into my eyes, and we connect beyond words. All is known between us now; you feel relieved and horny and excited and submissive. You feel cared for and loved and dominated, and a thousand more emotions. You utter a heartfelt low groan and hiss as you feel the silent pop—and it's in. It's sliding deep and full and hard into you. Your ass is filled with hard cock, and your breath is coming out in shuddering gasps. I straighten and you feel the push of my hips; I am all the way in. Your ass is filled, your ass is taken. I lean down and my chest presses on your breasts; you feel the clothespins again. My lips brush on yours, and my eyes are sparkling fire. My lips press hard and force your willing mouth open; my tongue is hard in your mouth. I take your mouth, and you kiss back with your own passion. Your arms move to hold me but strain helplessly instead, bound by the ropes. You whimper, frustrated, into my mouth, crying out in pleasure as you feel the slow, sliding strokes of cock beginning to fuck your ass.

My biceps press on your bound wrists and ankles as my chest takes up the space between your spread thighs. I wedge in and lift and press down as I slowly fuck your ass. I bring my hands up close and touch my fingertips gently on your face. You see the patience and concentration in my eyes; my jaw is firm, and my mouth is cocked in a half-smile. Your eyes are soft and knowing and needy; your face goes slack at times as I work my cock deep into your ass. I take your ass, and it's a biological thing, a sexual thing, a physical and emotional thing; as you are naked and bound on your dining-room table and your man is having you as you have longed to be had, your breaths are held and released and drawn in. Our eyes continue to talk and sparkle and caress one another, as worries and doubts fade. The imagined discussions are no longer needed.

Our lips and eyes locked, you are surrendered and submissive and complete. You feel intensely your worth to yourself and to us, and you kiss back with a sudden, hard passion. You are rewarded with a heated passion that has tripled in my eyes. You feel waves of pleasure as the thick cock slides slowly and tenderly within. Your ass shifts smoothly into the cock you have been waiting for. As the momentum and the force of the thrusts increases, you push your body in short, thudding shoves. You feel both frightened and orgasmic deep, deep in your ass. Your eyes close, your mouth opens, and your pussy, swollen and juicy, is ready to cum from your ass-fucking. You are so dirty, and the act is so intimate, your eyes mist over. As you stare up at me all woman and little girl and sensual goddess, I feel my cock grow even harder. I go deeper into your tight-glove warmth with every stroke, your face goes slack and your body grows tense. Coiled and pre-orgasmic again, I see your eyes go smoky and piercing and knowing and beautiful as your jaw suddenly tightens. My hand flies quickly to your pussy, and as my finger finds your clit, you arch your back and close your eyes; you cum again.

After your last orgasm, you are utterly spent. On your back on your dining-room table, breathing deeply in the glow, you revel it in all. Your mind processes the experience as you enjoy the lazy, pleasured spasms as they fade within you. You feel my hands on your wrists and the ropes, and you open your eyes a bare crack to see me. I stand between your legs as I release the knots. I let the rope fall to the table, and the look in my eyes tells you everything you need to know. I lay my adoring and worshipful hands on your wrist and ankle; unbound, your legs move apart. I begin to untie the other rope with the same gentle care; your chest tightens, and in this unguarded moment, my devotion and adoration of you is evident in every touch and caress of my hands on your skin. Your arms go to your sides flat on the table. Your knees are up; you are laying there naked and sexed. I am above you and everything is right, so very right.

You start to get up. You are on one elbow, but then you see the look in my eyes, and your stomach flutters. You watch me as I turn away and bend down, and you hear the bag rustle for a moment before I stand up and step back, a thick black handle in my grip. You then see a thin length of leather hanging from the handle. You watch me jog the whip once, twice; the end of the whip moves and dances just above the floor. I see your body tighten, and you feel your pulse race. At the sight of the black leather whip in my strong, masculine hand, your stomach flip-flops and your pussy twinges, thrumming rubber-band taut and tingly. As you stare at the whip in my hand, you feel more vulnerable and helpless and horny with each passing moment.

I hike the handle up in my grip and draw the cock-hard leather the length of your slit. I press the handle just inside the swollen, puffy lips and rock the handle slowly up and down. The top of the handle comes down and presses on your clit mound. Lifting it up only slightly before you feel the base of the whip handle touch, I touch into your dripping cunt hole and smile as the slow seesaw of smooth rolled leather pressed on your throbbing clit and your spasming, juicy hole. It's so lewd and so right, I can barely see straight.

"Ohhh fuck, you're gonna cum, you're gonna cum," I tease. "Now get off that table. Now. You know you don't belong there."

I step back, and the handle is suddenly gone from your pussy. There is no orgasm. You look up, but there are no concerned and caring eyes close to yours. There is no helping you cum. I stand back from you with the whip, holding it up, low and dangling and threatening and ready. You heard an order, and you are responding. Your eyes are down, you nod and quickly get yourself down off the table.

"On all fours. You crawl. Do your hear me?"

Your mind can barely form words as your body thrums with a new and overwhelming fire. You are about to nod, but you wince instead at the sudden and incredibly loud crack of the whip. It sounds like it is right next to your head; in a panic, you drop down and get to all fours. You look up in honest shock, and I am standing calmly a few steps back, holding the whip. I look down at you with a cold intensity that takes away the last of your vanilla you; your insides turn to jelly, your rational mind fades, and your submissive mind emerges clear and wanting and willing.

You are down on your hands and knees, and your arms shake slightly. Your stomach tight and queasy, you look up into my eyes, and that look is still there. You have never felt more *naked* than you do right now, never felt more *exposed* than you feel in this moment, here in your own dining room. For the man you love and married, the man who loves you, you crawled off the table like an errant pet. For him, you felt your vanilla cover break apart, disintegrate, and fade away as you went down to the floor on the order of the same voice that over pillows this morning, asked about your day ahead. When your wife-and-mother with her vanilla desires façade was all he knew about, when your "other" needs were still your very deep secret (or so you thought), things were different—until lunchtime today when he came home and things changed so suddenly. The table and the rope and cumming, and now this? Naked and ordered about and crawling?

"Crawl your ass over to me and kiss my balls—now—or you will feel this."

You look at me with serious eyes, wide with shock, and you nod. So many boundaries and lines have just been crossed and trampled, so many doors have opened at the same time for you, you can only nod again and lower your head, trying to process this new experience. As you move your arms and begin to crawl slowly over to me, you ready yourself to kiss the balls of a man very ready to use that whip.

"Kneel … that's it."

The tone of voice is now warm and encouraging, and you feel a rush of relief inside. On your knees now, you breathe out, lean forward, and purse your lips.

Suddenly, my hand is on the top of your head, and you feel a sting as your hair is gripped and pulled and your face and lips are moved tight to my balls and ball sack. Your eyes blink and close and open again, your mouth open slack in surprise. Your head is tilted back and my hand is at your mouth, and I force my balls, cum-heavy and large, into your mouth.

"I arranged for the kids to stay the night at your sister's," I say wickedly. "She said she hopes you and I do something fun."

The voice above you is warm and calm and so familiar as your mouth is stuffed with balls like a common whore. You look up, uncertain and shaking and completely aroused. I look down at you as I speak, and I nod and move your head with the fistful of your hair in my hand. You feel the balls lodge themselves even more fully in your mouth.

"I told her we would be doing something a little different. She liked that."

Your eyes soften and calm and for a moment, and you forget the balls in your mouth that round out your cheeks. You watch me as I put the whip down. My hand disappears behind me and returns with a black leather crop. After you feel my hand release from your hair and my balls pull out of your mouth, you sink back on your calves and look up at me.

"And by 'something a little different' … start crawling to the kitchen."

You lower your eyes and take in one more glance of my cock; it is hard and thick and pointing straight up. You are seeing it differently now.

Suddenly and without warning, you feel a sting that instantly turns to white-hot heat on your ass cheek. Confused, you register the crack of leather as it fills the room. You begin to crawl, quickly and awkwardly, toward the kitchen. As you crawl, you tense and arch your back your back downward, just as a second point of red-hot pain explodes on your ass. You cry out, half-stumbling, and move yourself forward onto the cool linoleum. As a third and fourth crack of the leather sears your skin, you crawl blindly, hands touching on the cabinet doors beneath the sink, the bottom of the refrigerator, and the floor again. The whisper-swish and the sudden crack and the biting pain of the crop find its mark as you desperately try to get away from it.

"Stop."

Your momentum comes to an awkward stop; your ragged breath struggles to escape, and your skin is on striped fire. You lower your head and wince, biting on your lip for a moment before raising your head up.

"You did very well for me. You have some nice lines."

With great effort, you hold yourself still for me. You try to understand what is happening. You watch the bottoms of my slacks as I walk slowly around you, you listen to my words and the relaxed tone of my voice, and the hum of the refrigerator. It's all too much, too much at once and yet, not enough. Your skin burns in a hundred places, your hands and knees are sore, but you can't ignore your body's response to this assault. Your nipples are rock hard and your pussy is swollen with a huge orgasm that is still deep down but demanding to happen. You wonder if you have any control of your body left, and then you feel my hand on the back of your neck. It urges you down; the only direction is down, and you go down obediently; your cheek and head and shoulders go down to the floor. The hand is there for just a moment, and then it is gone. You feel the cool floor on the side of your face on the floor, and you breathe out, glancing up with your eyes. You say nothing and hold back a whimper as my hands slide down and cup your ass cheeks. *No, no … please,* you think, but you are helpless to resist. Slowly and surely, I spread your ass cheeks open, and the first touch of the room air on your rosebud and pussy makes you cringe inside with a mix of humiliation and shame. The orgasm hard and throbbing in your cunt and it wants to cum, badly.

Your head and arms on the tiled floor and your ass lewdly up, I hear your deep breathing as I walk over to the porch way. You watch me step out, and you hear a rattling, rummaging noise, one you're quite familiar with now. You place the noise just as I walk back in, and your eyes go straight to the clothespins I hold in my hand.

You mumble quietly, "Oh no, no, hon …" as I go to one knee by your side. Suddenly, roughly, my other hand goes on your breast, and I bend it. You feel the jab of wood and a cool sting as the clothespin snaps down on your nipple. Your nipple warms quickly to a red-hot, fiery, pinching bite; you glance down at your breast and catch a glimpse of the clothespin tight on your nipple. You feel my hand on your other breast, followed by a quick, rough, pulling grab. You feel the wood push and press at you, and you turn your head in response to the same cool sting and the same fiery biting pain. Your nipple is clamped tightly, and your head is down. Your eyes are misty, your face red, and your mind races in an attempt to process what is happening. You slide even deeper into submission, your pussy puffy, swollen, and screaming for hard, sadistic cock. You can't believe you just thought that, and you chide yourself. Even as you arch your back downward and you feel your ass cheeks spread and your pussy stretch for a merciful bit of relief, you are shocked by your impertinence. You feel a hand on each cheek and then fingers, sloppy and rude and probing, enter your ass crack. You feel a finger on each side press, and you are staring hard at nothing, wide-eyed and quiet. As the two fingers get themselves unhurried and forceful into your asshole and then deep into your ass, you hold back a whimper. You bite on your lower lip as the fingers pull apart your asshole and stretch it. They slip out and rub on the wrinkled pucker of your rosebud and force themselves in knuckle-deep. You feel your ass spasm, and your held-back breath bursts suddenly from your lungs. Your pussy drips now, and you feel yourself push back on the fingers. The fingers go in deeper, and you groan with pleasure and press your face to your arms. You are suddenly mortified but so turned on you can barely think. You take it all because you want to please me. Your knees slide outward, and as your ass goes back and spreads out even more, the heat of humiliation washes over your face.

"Ohhh-Godddd-unhhh."

You feel the fingers slide out and leave your ass as you breathe out a shuddering breath. You slide your hands back toward you and press them down hard. You feel my hand on the crack of your ass. At the sudden fullness of my thumb press-sliding into your ass, you feel yourself being lifted slightly. Your knees go light as your hips and ass are raised up. As you feel the wide, firm hand slide down over your dripping, messy mound, your mind says *diaper,* and you cringe with embarrassment as a finger cruises slowly up and down your slit. It's so welcome, so needed, and so gentle in your pussy, the momentary release of tension brings tears to your eyes. Your eyes close and your mouth slacks from the waves of pleasure surging up from your pussy. The thumb in your ass becomes bearable as the finger moves up and down on your pussy. You need cock, but the finger moves up instead. You feel the tip hunting for your clit as the thumb lifts you higher still. You feel like a helpless little girl—and you don't care. The slick tip finds your clit, and your clit is being fingered by your man, the man who knows you best, who now knows the submissive you are. Your eyes tear up again, and it's been a relief, such a relief. Your needs are now revealed—and he knew all along, he just knew. You close your eyes as your orgasm wells up under his gentle fingertip, and you cum, your mind blank of all thought or fantasy, your body racked from the intensity, and your smile is deep and serene.

CHAPTER 26

Chair

You hear the door, and you get up off the couch. You've already changed into a nice casual shirt and jeans. You purse your lips and shag your hands through your hair for a last-minute primp. You look in the direction of the kitchen and the back door, your face casual. You look forward to the "Welcome home, babe. How was your day?" exchange. Your pussy is a tight, throbbing mess. Your stomach is tight—oh, be honest, your whole body is tight and tingling after a day of work and being strong and putting up with shit. You look at the entryway to the kitchen and already you want to kneel before me. You already want cock, already want to be ravished and fucked and loved. Knowing that you are going to get all of that makes your knees genuinely and truthfully weak; your pussy is a horny, juicy puff between your legs, and it wants to be split and stuffed with hard cock—my hard cock. You are mesmerized by your pussy's needs and your mind at the same time. With a knowing, nervous, horny-girl smirk and giggle, your nipples go rock hard and tender all at once. They nudge the inside of your T-shirt, eager for abuse. Your deep cunt twinges enough that you almost have to walk bowlegged. Abuse done right is a glorious thing, and God, but you love that word. You touch the tip of your tongue to your lip and get to the kitchen.

When you turn the corner and step into the room, you see me. I put my briefcase down on the table, my white shirt sleeves half rolled up on my forearms, my chest visible under the shirt. I hang the suit jacket on the chair, and you get a glimpse of my tight ass in the straight lines of the charcoal-gray slacks. When you glance down and see the black wingtip dress shoes, you feel a soft twinge in your gut. You look up you look for the belt and the belt buckle, and you swallow and get your face set back to casual.

"Hey, you. How was your day?"

I look up at you and smile a grateful smile, the smile that is yours. My face is relaxed and warm, and you shudder because it does at these moments of connection we share.

"Long one. How was yours?"

You start to answer; your mouth is moving, and you are replying with something, but your eyes are on mine. We have skipped ahead; your eyes sparkle like mine and you know it's coming. You reply, and I listen. Then I say something, but the room is already hot, way too hot. I am at you, and you are in my arms. We continue to talk without listening, our tender, needful, urgent kisses hold all of the meaning and set the tone.

The tension grows in the heat as we kiss and my hands go to your shirt. Your arms go up as we kiss; I to love kiss your cheek.

"You are a beautiful, beautiful woman, baby," I say sincerely.

I pull your shirt up and over your face, and it's out of the way. I look down at your succulent, full breasts, and I breathe out hard. I go to your neck in a lustful rush, kissing you hard as our hands meet. I go to your crotch to get your jeans open; as your hands ease down on the sides, I bring my hands to touch the sweet, fucking softness of your lower back before I slide my hands flat and tight over your perfect ass cheeks. You mewl quietly, a whimper so womanly, so strong, and so loaded with sexual ease, it overwhelms me. I swallow hard and bury my face in your hair. I breathe you in. As your hands touch my shirt sleeves, I bring my hands up to the small of your ass cheeks and squeeze them fiercely. I slide my fingertips around to the touch your moist cunt and brush them against the swollen folds of your labia. I move over into the viscous, sweet wetness of your slit, of your petal-soft skin, and my fingers dig into your aching cunt. You kiss at my face and lay your head on my shoulder, as your hands slide and grip my shoulders, wanting more. Your legs straight, your jeans easily slide down and bunch, and you side kick them away. You press yourself to me and mold yourself to my chest. My greedy, rude fingers crawl into your surrendering, aching pussy, and you look up at me, sudden and strong and in need of submission. Our eyes meet for a moment, and your face changes subtly. I can see the trust in your eyes as you go to my ear and mouth the words. Your moans, soft and throaty, thrill me. As four fingers of each hand wedge-hump your dripping pussy, you press your tits to the crisp white of the shirt, and your nipples tingle-thrum. Your hand brushes over the hardness of the belt buckle, and you moan again as you kiss my neck.

"Ohhhhh, yes sir," you say under your breath, as my hands go to the tops of your shoulders and urge you down.

Once down, your face presses on my shirt, and you kiss along the way as you go to your knees. Your lips brush against the metal of the belt buckle as your movement slows to a stop. Your hands go to my hips. As you kiss the zipper flap, you feel the cock bulging underneath, and you lick at the fabric. As you bring your hands over, you feel my hands press on yours. You whimper-whisper as you are eased further down.

You lower your head, and it's only the beginning. You hear movement behind you, and you turn your head to see a glimpse of chrome and a glimpse of yellow. You lift yourself to your knees and turn to look. You kneel without moving. As I place the chair in the center of the kitchen, you swallow and look at the chrome metal legs and the yellow plastic seat. It's the lone chair left from an old kitchen set, and you remember how we both laughed when we saw it at that tag sale. It was the lone chair on the grass, the paper tag showing fifty cents. We both smile at the memories—the way you went to move on and I didn't, the way you paused as I went closer to the chair and put my hands on it, the way you pressed and checked the chair out and talked to the woman running the tag sale. The way I handed her the money and hoisted the chair with one hand, the joke of a chair embarrassingly yellow and kitschy; the way I came to you and we stood there for a moment, and you asked "What the fuck?", all smiles; the way I kissed you quickly on your cheek, leaned in close, and whispered, "I told you to say hi to your new Titty Chair," with a steady, dead-serious look in my eyes that only you saw. And the way your pussy melted to butter slop as we stood together in the front yard of somebody's house with the big tree and the sidewalk and that card table with that crap on it and little tags everywhere and other people milling around us.

As you sit on the chair now, you are naked, your dry-wet thighs pressed together, and your hands on your lap. I go to the back door and come back and drop the cloth bag on the countertop. My hand, big and rude, digs into the bag and comes out with a fistful of clothespins. I drop them in a pile, and they scatter on the counter. You sit straight up, your back pressed against the plastic. You stare at me and take it all in; it's happening so quickly, you feel sparks of humiliation as little girl and cocksucker and pain whore. Yes, you are my pain whore, and as you stare as my hand calmly arranges the pins, you bite on your lower lip, your stomach going tight and fluttery and your pulse beginning to race.

The chair—the Titty Chair; *your* Titty Chair. I smile now at the memory of how I first handed you the chair and the way I made you carry the chair, the seat up and in front, the back held close to your body, my whispered command to pull the chair in tight, tighter, until your breasts were mashed and bulging out, ridiculous and awkward, the metal and back of the chair dead center in your chest and your elbows out as you discreetly but obviously strained to keep that chair mashed into your chest. And then the way I kept us continuing to browse, the way I stopped and looked at things I was never going to buy, and the way other people and husbands and wives looked at you as you held that chair, so ridiculously tight to your body. In your mind (and you were sure, theirs too), it was so obviously deviant and perverted. The way you tried not to return their looks, and when you did, the puzzled looks from some, including the sort-of -knowing looks from the guys and yes, the knowing looks from other women. These looks turned your pussy to a ripe, swollen fruit as you stood there unable to move, not allowed to move, your pussy bloating with juice and threatening to wet your tight jeans. I smile at the memory of the envious guys who continued to look over at you from all parts of the yard—as well as the calm stares of the wives. These stares owned you as the waves of humiliation caused you to physically shake as you strained and tried to cope. As I took my sweet fucking time looking at that fucking pile of paperbacks, your hands gripped your Titty Chair tightly to your chest, and they grew sweaty on the chrome tubing of that stupid chair.

I look down at the clothespins arranged in a long, neat row, and my hands go to the front of my jeans. As I find and open my belt, my hand grips the buckle. You watch, paralyzed, as I get the belt out; I move behind you, and you see a blur of black and feel the wide press on your neck. Your head goes back slightly as the belt is pulled, the end is threaded, and the loop is made. One more tug and the loop grows tight and snug around your neck. The hand comes around, and the leather belt leash is dropped down between the dark-red punks of your swollen, hard nipples and the sweaty globes of your breasts.

I come to your front, and you look up at me. I point down at the chair, and you know to stay. You nod, barely, and still stare at me. I walk off without acknowledging you; you see me go to the back door and go outside. You swallow and breathe out and look down at the floor, your pussy gripped tight on the hard nut of a forming orgasm. You force yourself to look up, to look around the kitchen. You are naked and leashed as you sit on a chair bought at a tag sale. You said you loved it. Now, all you can think of is your thighs and ass, your pussy a wet whore mess of juicy on the plastic seat. You *could* get up. You *could* end this. You *could* get up and clean this up. Your hands grip the sides of the chair, and you have to lift yourself slightly. The forming orgasm that wells up embarrasses you, but you ride it out. Ride the crest and then silently talk it down. You sit back down, leashed and exposed; your heart pounds, and you just want more of this. *You sick fuck,* you condemn yourself silently. You bite your lip again. *Oh you sick, sick fucker.* The door opens, and I come back in. At the sight of the coiled rope in my hands, you tighten all over. In the next moment, I am at you. I hold the rope a few feet up and let the end dangle down in front of you. I grab your left tit and wrap the rope tightly, neatly around it. You look at the rope as it is wound three times around your other tit. I finish with a big loop around both tits. It is my turn to take it all in—the loose hair, the tight weave of the rope, the golden brown and the smell of it your rope-burned breasts. They are numb and turning dark red. You look up to see my intense eyes and unsmiling face, and then down at the rope that binds your tits. You need to lift yourself, you need to lift up as another orgasm wells up again.

"Oh my God, God, ohhh God—"

You watch as I turn to the counter and turn back to you, a nipple clamp in my hand. It is made of chrome, and you can see the very heft of it in my hand. You mouth *oh fuck* as the clamp slams down on your dark-pink nipple. The jaws open, and I see you eyeing it fearfully.

"The fucking metal? Yes, bitch, look at the fucking metal." I look up, instantly annoyed. "Fucking hair clips? Are you kidding me? Your nipples need real pain. Your nipples need to cum, baby."

I open the jaws and trap your plump, trembling nipple within. At the sudden snap and the searing, biting heat, you hump up and arch your back. When the clamp opens, you fall back down, gagging on your own spit and almost cum. I release the spring handles again, and the clamp bites again. You key up and arch up hard as the clamp opens. You fall back, tears in your eyes as the clamp closes, and you edge again. Your elusive orgasm is like a steel football in your gut. You lose track of time as the clamp closes and opens and closes and opens. It bruises and bites and tortures you, and you can't hold back the inevitable another moment more.

"Ohhhhhh fuck …unnh—ohhh!"

The clamp metal bites and cuts at you, and in the brace of the white-hot pain and cold-heat torture, you cum. Your arms shoot straight and lock; your knees slowly and bend as you go into a squat; you flood the chair and the floor with your gushing juices. The clamp bites through your nipple, and you embrace your nature: you whore, you fucking slut-whore, fuck yes. Through the orgasm, your teeth grind dangerously, your jaw tightens perilously, and you hold your upper body as still as you can, but you cannot deny the orgasms that come one after the other. Was it two or three or ten at once? Until I remove the clamp, there is no break for you. I snap the last one off and walk off, leaving you gasping, crying without tears, your dirty mind fucked clear.

CHAPTER 27

Coupons

You are sitting at the kitchen table, a cup of coffee to the side, coupons spread out around you. Saturday mornings, you like to clip coupons and then head out to get the grocery shopping done before the stores fill up.

With a neat pile of coupons to your left and the scraps to your right you pick up the scissors and place them next to the coupons. You reach for your coffee, cold now, and take a sip, sighing as you take a closer look at the coupons. That's a two-for-one on the detergent.

I come into the room, dressed, you notice. You're a little surprised that I'm in a T-shirt and jeans and that I showered. Looking good, different from my usual Saturday morning mix of shorts, bed hair, and stubble.

"Hi, babes," you say. "You're up early."

"I am? Yeah, I guess I am."

The tone—you hear it, watching me from your coupons as I look around casually for a coffee cup.

"Are you going out this morning?" you ask. "You look like you are. I'm going grocery shopping in a little bit. I can pick up what you want, save you a trip—"

"Nope. Not going anywhere."

You knew the answer to your question before you asked it. Your chest tightens; your pulse beginning to race. You look down at your coupons without really seeing them as you feel me moving behind you, and you hear the cupboard open. I must be getting a cup.

"Well, I'd like to hang out with you, babes, but I gotta get my butt out of here. Hopefully I can get a good parking spot."

A silk binding lands on the pile of scraps. You were expecting something. You feel yourself jump without moving, startled, holding yourself still. You have a moment to look at the binding before a second strip of silk lands to your left, draping itself over the pile of coupons.

You don't say anything. Your mind is racing, and there's a flutter in your stomach, a vague tingling in your pussy.

"You need me to take those to the dry cleaners for you?" You manage to get the words out, meant to sound mildly joking and sarcastic. Your voice is as calm as before but a little softer, a little tighter. You don't turn your head, staring at the smooth, white strips of cloth, your nipples hardening.

"No, no, that's okay."

My voice is calm too, but with that subtle shift in tone that goes straight to the center of your mind and your cunt.

You watch my hand come over your shoulder to pick up the binder and then feel my other hand on your wrist, gently but firmly lifting it and guiding your arm toward the back of the chair. Then the coolness of the silk, wrapping around, securing your wrist to the back of the chair.

You swallow, remaining still as the other strap is picked up from the table and your wrist is lifted, brought down behind you, and secured.

My lips graze on your neck with soft kisses.

I grab on to the front of your T-shirt, tightening my fist until the neckline and the bottom of the thin shirt are together.

I calmly reach down for the scissors you were using earlier and cut the shirt with one neat stroke, tossing the scissors on the table before pulling the shirt to the sides to expose your breasts.

You are looking at me, your eyes steady. You bite on your lower lip.

I reach into the pocket of my jeans and pull out the clamp—shiny, compact, partially hidden by my hand. You know what it is without looking, but you glance anyway, a thump and a twinge deep in your gut.

You watch as I hold the clamp up for a moment, looking at it. Then, without hesitation, I bring the clamp down to your hard nipple. The metal is smooth and hard as you watch and feel it being fitted, feel it pressing onto your nipple, and then the sudden metal pinching, tightness. I stand back, casually looking down at the clamp, not at you.

I reach down and grab your breast, squeezing it tightly, and then use my other hand to turn the clamp tighter, watching the squeezed nipple turn a deep red.

Satisfied, I step back to look at you your arms straight down at your sides, your wrists tied tight to the chair, your T-shirt cut and open, your breasts exposed. The dark red of your nipple inside the metal of the clamp; your other breast, the nipple hard and waiting. I see the look on your face, the sincerity of the sub starting to show in your eyes, the look of need, the trying-to-be-calm look. Even as I know your pussy is thrumming, tingling, getting wet and then wetter; how aware and turned on you are by the delicious, lewd perviness of slipping into sub mode, tied to the kitchen chair in your own kitchen.

I casually reach into my jeans pocket and pull out the second clamp, pretending not to notice your stare as I calmly grab your other breast in a tight trip and force the clamp onto your nipple. I corkscrew it roughly down until the already-darkening tip of your nipple shows. A strong pulse of pleasure spikes from your pussy as I tighten the clamp far too much, painfully reducing the size of the sensitive nub. You feel a sudden physical weakness as the pain and your pussy take over and cover you in a warm rush of pleasure. Your mind slips deep into the mode, the last of your other thoughts fading away as the fantasies take over. Almost in a slow blur, I pass close to you. You take in the scent of me, the manliness of me, so powerful your cunt aches for my thick, hard, pulsing cock—soft kisses and cuddling.

As I lean close to you, your face is less than an inch from my chest and shoulder. I reach down to the first clamp and tighten it several more turns, feeling the sharp metal teeth sinking into the soft raspberry flesh.

I leave your side abruptly, pretending not to hear your soft, mewling whimper or see the open, half-pleading innocence in your eyes as you look up at me. I casually pour a cup of coffee and sit down in the other chair across from you. I pick up a section of the paper and begin to read it.

You feel another wave of pleasure tremors wash over you, your submissive mind in full, watching the way I sit there, calm and in control. You feel the sharp needle pain on your rock-hard nipples and your aching, horny cunt, embarrassingly wet. You should be clipping coupons, drinking coffee, but the other you is here now, tied and exposed, subbie. Yes, so fucking wet. Aroused but at the same time feeling oddly embarrassed, you feel the clamps tight on your nipples and feel a slight amount of humiliation that your breasts are exposed here in the kitchen while I sit there, fully clothed. You subconsciously go to lift your hands, to try to close your shirt to cover yourself and feel the ropes that are binding your wrists sending another thrumming tingle through your pussy. God, so wet. Your two minds struggle, but the rational you is losing to the submissive you. God, you are sure your panties are soaked by now.

I lift my cup and finish my coffee, put it down, and fold the paper neatly on itself before pushing back the chair and getting up, just like any other Saturday. You watch, emotional, your pussy aching. How can I just ignore you?

Without looking at you, I turn away from the table and appear to be walking right past you. You look at my now-empty seat, tears forming in your eyes.

But I stop next to you. You turn your head to look at me, allowing yourself a small smile.

You see my hand, large and inches from your face, lowering my zipper, unbuttoning the stud, opening my jeans, and yanking them down a little before reaching in and easing out my half-hard cock. You stare closely at the slit of the purplish mushroom head, less than an inch from your lips. You glance up, just once, to see me looking down far above you and then back down at the thick cock. You know there is no question, no doubt, that you are going to suck cock.

Your vision is blocked by my face. I bring my lips to yours and kiss you deeply. Your yelp of surprise is muffled as I continue the kiss, my tongue passionately forcing itself into your mouth.

You groan into my mouth as you feel my fingertips finding and working under the band of your terrycloth shorts. You whimper as you feel my stiff fingers sliding down and spreading your wet slit, feeling up your soaked, horny pussy mound.

I pull my mouth back. You moan softly, needing my lips and tongue. I place gentle, affectionate kisses on your neck while roughly but calmly manhandling your hungry cunt.

You cry out in lustful pleasure as I slide two stiff fingers hard up into your clutching tightness. You squirm hard on the chair, trying desperately to grind your pussy down on the stiff thickness, trying to cum.

I pull my hand away abruptly, up and out of your shorts. You feel the already-soaked fabric snap back and press against the wetness of your dripping cunt.

You groan loudly, your eyes closed. So hot, so fucking ready to cum, your nipples on fire. You feel my finger under your chin, gently but firmly lifting. You open your eyes and find yourself staring into the pinkish slit. You stare, your mouth slack open. That cock looks so fucking good.

You feel my other hand on the back of your head in the same instant you see my fingers circling the shaft. The momentary feel of the soft flesh of the wide head passes your lips, and the sudden fullness in your mouth, the sudden filling hardness pressing down your tongue, grazing the roof of your mouth, touching the back of your throat. Your mind blanks as you try to process the cock blatantly taking ownership of your mouth, your mind and pussy begging for more.

My hand is on the back of your head, the black hair on stomach muscles. The totally present feeling of cock meat fills your mouth and presses against your throat. The electric, sexy tension connects between your mouth and throat, your burning numb nipples, and your wide open, wet, and waiting pussy. You are a sexy mess of tingling, sensitive tits and a horny, aggressive cunt. Your face, mouth, and throat are fully occupied and owned by the thick, hard cock that is making your rock-hard clit thrum painfully and your everyday do-good, weakly protesting mind go completely sub.

Chapter 28

Bored

You're walking around the house, looking for something to do, for something else to think about. My body and my eyes and my cock are on your mind, your pussy tingling and swollen and begging for your fingers. You sit down on the couch and turn on the TV, flipping through the channels and looking at the walls and seeing yourself up against that one, my hand tight in your hair, and your cheek against the wall, your back arched and your ass back, your legs straight and locked and shaking. My fingers finding and gripping the band of your shorts, my other hand too, and your shorts yanked down to the curve of your ass cheeks and then another tug down to your thighs. The room air on your nakedness, your pussy throbbing, the sudden hard softness of cock head touching on your juicy, wet pussy, and the muscled up-and-down rough plowing that lights your pussy and body on fire. My hands wide and tight on your hips and the sudden stretching thickness of cock spearing itself smooth and deep into your tight, spasming cunt. Your hands slam flat on the wall, and your back arches your pussy back into the muscled, slow-thrusting cock pole. Your eyes squint, and your mouth goes slack, touching your forehead to the wall as the waves of pleasure roll up your body and crash in your mind. Your pussy grip slides on rock-hard cock and turns to mush as you cry out and feel the wisps and tingles of orgasms forming up huge and demanding to happen.

Your breasts touch my chest, and our lips graze hard as we talk. You feel my hands firm on your hips and grip on the band of your sweats. The tug as I yank your sweats down midthigh, and you are staring into my eyes, knowing you have made my cock rock hard. A second tug, and your sweats are down to your knees. You feel the rough grab of my hand on your panties over the swollen, thrumming, wet mess of your pussy, and you are turned around, pushed to the bed, hands and knees. You straighten your arms and glance back at my hand on my jeans, and the hand and zipper coming down. Both of my hands are working the stud. The jeans open up wide, and the thick cock boner juts up and bobs, the split halves and dark slit of the purplish head. You lick at your lips as you feel the head touching your cunt, plowing up and down and up and down. Your head goes to the pillow as you feel the strong hands grip your hips, the sudden searing stretch and your breath stopping as your pussy is stuffed in a single muscled lunge. The head touches at the opening of your cervix, and your pussy stretches condom tight on the sliding pole of meat.

You go to your forearms and cry out, biting your lip and arching your back down, raising your bare ass and pussy and pushing back. You're taking the hard cock to the base and feeling the tap of balls and ball sack on your pussy before the hands go to your ass cheeks and push. You breathe out hard as the cock withdraws, unsheathes itself from your gripping wetness. The head catches in your cunt petals, and you are empty in the moment before you press your face into the pillow and groan. There's hard cock deep in your cunt again and withdrawing and spearing deep, finding new depth with each stroke before going into a slow, purposeful pistoning that is turning your pussy into mush. You feel the finger hunting and finding your tingling, aching clit, the measured cock strokes, and the pussy-slick ball of my middle finger working your hard clit back and forth, expert and knowing.

Your cheek is on the pillow, eyes closed, breathing hard, wincing as the cock thrusts bottom out deep inside you. Your clit hood is shelled back, and the exposed hard nub of your clit is bullied under the gliding finger zeroed in on top of it. You swallow hard and gasp and take it, the wisps and tremors of forming orgasms hushing your breath as the cock continues to pound. Your clit is sending voltage spikes directly to the center of your brain; your eyes are opening wide and closing half-lidded and opening fully as a muscled arm comes down near you. The hand grabs at a pillow, drags it over, and stuffs it roughly under your stomach. As the arm lifts away and you feel the hand on your ass cheek, the other hand is below, fingering your clit and the cock fucking you. You feel the hand on your cheek slide down between your slightly spread cheeks. You lift your head and lower it as you feel two fingertips dabbing lightly, rubbing on the sides of your ass crack before sliding down to touch and explore around your asshole. Your eyes close tight as you feel a fingertip tracing around the wrinkly, puckered skin and a sudden quivery shiver as the fingertip touches and presses in the center.

The fingertip is pressed and holding, snugged in the center of your asshole without entering. You feel pinned down, paralyzed. The cock moves your body slightly, and your asshole insinuates itself on the unmoving fingertip. Your arms go out straight, and your hands blindly grip on the sheets. You press your face down in the pillow and push back, feeling the hardness of the finger and your asshole opening around it. Your face warms, and you bring your arm back to subconsciously hide in it as you push back with your hips and cringe, red-faced and pleasured. Moaning again, you feel your asshole stretching around and sliding down on the finger and the queasy tingle of the finger entering your ass. Your ass and pussy are on mellowed fire now, the pistoning cock slowing to a rowing, broad-shouldered, old-school deep fuck. Your rational mind is fading, your thoughts and pleasures simplifying and intensifying to a pure, primal state. This is it, fucking, the fuck, the sex you've been craving, unhurried and good, so fucking good.

CHAPTER 29

Cubicle

The monthly reports for the third quarter—you look at the folders on your computer screen and the files on the desk and you sigh. *Paperwork.* Luckily, you were able to use this cubicle for the day. It's kind of a hike from where you usually sit, and there's no one else around to talk to, but whatever. It lets you get the job done quicker and get the hell out of here.

You move your large coffee to the side, and you settle in, clicking on folders and opening pages, getting into what needs to be done. At one point, you think you hear the door, and you pause, but it's quiet. You shrug and get your hand on the mouse and get back into the three documents and the manifest open on the screen in front of you.

"Hi."

You look up, startled but not badly, into the piercing eyes of an older man. His salt-and-pepper hair is neatly groomed, and he's clean shaven. You can't help but note how well his suit hangs. By his briefcase and the pharmaceutical pin on his lapel, you know he's a salesman.

"Hi, how are you? Can I help you?" You swivel in your chair to face him, not bothering to get up. You deal with salesmen all the time, and this won't take long.

"I'm with Smith Warren. We ran a short clinical with your hospital three years ago, and we were looking for a few case histories that don't seem to be in the final oncology report."

You nod noncommittally, slightly bored with the request and frankly a little irritated at the interruption, but you say nothing and he continues. "Anyway, your boss at the front desk said you were back here working on files and you might be able to help me."

You manage a smile and nod, glancing at the coffee you brought in and feeling tired as you slowly turn your chair back to the computer and begin minimizing the pages to clear the screen. You are feeling tired and a little bummed, a little cranky. The dinner and dancing last night were fun, back to his place was working, the couch was fine, and the making out was rockin' big time before his nine-year-old daughter came out of her room complaining of a stomach ache and then threw up. That was the end of the date, not counting puke cleanup and the I'm-sorrys and I'll-call-yous and the drive home after that, where you gripped the wheel and pressed your legs tight and tried not to think of his cock ain your mouth and the taste and the sucking, the blow job that was so gonna happen.

"It would be in the March-May timeframe, if that helps."

You glance up and nod and begin clicking and searching, going through the motions while you let your mind clear from last night. You adjust your hips discreetly to move your now-tingling pussy off of the pants seam that is pressing on your panties. You swallow and breathe out and lean forward slightly, peering at the screen as you get down to business and search for real folders, files, headings, reports; folders, files, headings, reports; point and click, point and click, all the while chatting and listening as he points things out. But under it all, your mind is playing last night over and over, the way your guy was lying back in his jeans and your hand sliding casually up and down his leg as you both talked and laughed. Your fingertips touched occasionally on his growing bulge, and there was no doubt in either of your minds what was about to happen. You were kissing and chatting and hanging out and getting to know each other a little more, and his cock was getting huge under your frequently checking fingertips.

"Right there. I'm sorry, you passed it, right there."

Startled again out of your daydream, you nod and try to refocus your eyes. Then his hand is in front of your face, his finger pointing to the screen. You are moving the cursor to follow, listening to his directions and feeling the touch of his thigh on your shoulder as he leans in.

"Oh, of course, right there, the C112VT folder. Yeah, sorry."

"You seem preoccupied. Everything okay?"

You click the folder open and turn your head, and you are suddenly less than an inch from his zipper. The fabric on either side angles down and away and outward, and you realize in the same moment that you are staring at fabric pushed up and out by a boner, a big fucking boner at that. But your eyes are already going up quickly. The moment passes, and you are looking up into this guy's eyes, looking at him with your professional face. You didn't just have your face in his crotch, and his crotch isn't just an inch from your face right this instant. His tented pants and huge, obvious damned boner aren't rude and a tongue's length away. You seem to be the only one here concerned about it. He is talking to you about something, about the folder, *but come on already, kind sir. Your cock is hard and huge and right in my face, and you keep talking.*

"And with the cluster reports here and here, we should have enough to complete the study."

You turn your eyes slightly and see his hand at the screen. He is still talking and motioning, but you hear the sudden raspiness in his voice, and you see the slight shaking in his hand. You hear yourself agreeing and saying something, but you don't know what. You feel yourself moving your head and your cheek, touching the thin fabric bulge, and you don't know what or why the fuck you are doing this, but you swear you feel faint pulsing on your cheek before you pull away and your stomach tightens and flutters.

"G-good, good question. We, uh, we get asked that a lot. Yes, uh, let's see. Yes, that type of question a lot."

You've turned your head to the screen, and you say something else supportive and professional. When you go to turn your head back toward his crotch, your cheek barely brushes again, and you realize he has moved closer. As you continue to turn your face, the pants ridge looms as large as the middle of your face, and you see the threads, and you smell cologne. You don't turn away. God damn it, you should, you should. You brush the tip of your nose on the ridge instead. You hear his breath change, and your lips touch the fine-weave material and the cock ridge, wide and close. You open your mouth softly and press your lips to the ridge and quickly kiss and start to move away, but you linger and breathe in the cologne again. You brush your cheek across one more time before you look up. He is looking down at you with intense, tender, sensual eyes.

Your eyes locked, you whisper, "Wife?"

"Widowed."

With his whispered reply and his kind eyes and face, a hundred conversations pass between you, and an understanding is reached. A pact is made, and your hand comes up. Your fingers find the zipper tab, and you can't believe you are doing this, but the other part of you is calm and in control and lowering the zipper. You watch the tab lifted up, riding up the arch of the ridge like a toy train and then coming over the ridge and down. Your fingers are pinched, bringing it down to the bottom. The zipper sides have opened and parted, and you bring your hand up and go inside and touch his briefs. You feel the heat of his cock underneath, and you slide your hand up and find the band. Your other hand touches lightly on his hip as your fingers curl on the band. You pull it out and down enough to get your hand around and ease it out. The head catches on the top of the zipper opening as it clears, and then his cock is out. You lower your hand away and look for a moment at the thick, pinkish shaft of hard cock jutting straight up and the purplish head above the belt line. Your hands are sliding around the back of his hips. You stick out your tongue and lick before you bring your hand back and ease the cock down to line the head up, wide and waiting at your mouth. You lick the slit and taste him, taste his masculinity. You lick it once more quickly before you open your mouth and take him in.

Waiting

The talks, the discussions, that night making out on the couch with your face hidden on the side of my neck. Your soft kisses and whispered, confessed desires—not wanting to be on the Pill and why. That moment, that long moment, before my face turned to yours, my eyes finding yours, holding yours, nodding, and that soft kiss. And then the wait, the agreed-to three weeks that went to four as the Pill faded from your body and the feeling returned. The need, just as you wanted it to, just as you hoped it would, day by day and night by night. Getting dressed for work, and the tingling in your pussy as you slowly slipped your lace panties up your legs. The quick way you put your office slacks on and tucked in your blouse and tousled your hair. Slipping on your shoes and looking in the mirror and leaving the bedroom; your stomach going tight and fluttery as you passed the bed. All those spread knees, thick-cock orgasms, pussy-gripping times happen again in your mind. During the drive to work and time spent at work, you're occupying yourself and doing well, chatting with your group, very efficient and competent and smiling. All the while you're holding your pussy in, feeling every nerve, individually and together, talking to you, tugging your sleeve, oh by the way coy at times—sweet cajoling and then relentless. The clitoris and labia and the passage deep into your cunt demanding cock, hard cock, thick pole apple-headed, filling and stretching, all man and masculine and precumming; cum-laden balls heavy on your cunt hole with every thrust. Looking at the numbers on your computer screen, you're breathing out, looking away and around the room before lifting your coffee and taking a quick sip.

Then the end of the fourth week arrives, following that long Friday at work and coming home. It was time; going out and dinner plans not going to happen. Your work stuff is on the counter. You hear the back door, and you turn as I walk in. "Hey." A touch of your tongue to your lips, and our eyes meet. The sexual tension goes to almost unbearable for both of us.

"Hey, babe," I offer back. "I know we're not going out tonight."

You look so perfect and wanting and ready. My cock is rock hard as I put my briefcase down on the counter next to you and ease my arms around you, kissing you deeply and tenderly. Our faces are close and breathing hushed, full breaths. More kissing and speaking wordlessly. You look at me for a moment and thank me for waiting the month with you. Your hand brushes on the tented crotch of my slacks, and your breath catches. The pulsing thickness is just under the thin fabric—your man's cock with a month of need, a month of needing to fuck to release, to fuck you and your pussy. Your fingers dance slowly, urgently and on the balls, hanging huge and heavy. The yummy cum, oh God, the yummy cum.

The edge of the counter is behind you, and your hands come up. You put your arms around my neck and bring your loving lips close to mine, staring into the intense adoration you see in my eyes. You feel my hands on the front of your pants and my fingers on the buckle of the thin dress belt. The belt is being opened, the clasp undone, and your hands are touching mine as the zipper is yanked down hard. You are pulled toward me, your hands going hard into my hair as you feel your pants open and drop down. The kitchen air is cool on your thighs and the moist heat intimate in your panties. My hands are on both sides of your hips, and your panties go down. Your quick kisses, your eyes seducing and hopeful and sparkling. Your hands go back to my slacks and get the zipper down. Your hand goes in, and my hand is on yours. My whispers are hoarse on your neck as your fingers ease around the shaft and your fingertips touch the base and balls. You palm the head as you ease it out, guide it out. I am groaning and kissing, helpless and tender, on your ear as you glide your fingertips on the length of jutting shaft and touch the head. Your hand goes in all the way and down to find my balls, bringing them out and letting them drop, heavy and swollen, as you carefully tuck the open zipper of my slacks behind them.

My eyes close as I tilt my head and kiss you hard, my tongue entering your mouth in the same moment you feel my hands going warm and cupping your ass cheeks. Your pussy is pulsing and knotting and going to a wet mess as you feel balls on your labia. You feel the rounded, thick, pulsing warmth of the shaft pressing lengthy and animal on the soft skin of your stomach. The cock is so close, so close, and you want this so badly. I turn you around; you are stomach-tight to the edge of the counter, and you feel my hand on the back of your neck, gripping and urging you down. Your breasts touch the counter and then your face, down. You feel the touch of cock head going between your legs, inside your thighs, the sudden plowing separation of your swollen labia as the head and shaft pass up your slit in a single passing stroke. Your hands go flat and pressing, your forearms stiff, as your pussy grips, viscous and juicy, on the pole of hard bone wedging itself, jutting and lengthwise and pulsing in your slit. You lift yourself straight-armed and bite on your lip as cock finds your clit hood and throbbing clit and stays there; cock head pressing, shaft wedged between the lips. You moan out, silent and begging, to the countertop, crying out through gritted teeth as the angle shifts, as the cock, upright and pressing, goes perpendicular and spears deep into you with a straight-in muscled lunge that lifts you tiptoed and further onto the counter. Your pussy wedges down on the thick fence rail of rock-hard cock between your legs. Your breath is caught in your throat, and your pulse beats in your ears. Your breasts are tight beneath you.

My lips are suddenly, softly at your ear. "You are mine, all of you."

Your mind goes a hot, hot red.

I turn you to face me before I reach down and lift you easily into my arms, turning and walking us to the bedroom as we kiss in the low light of the bedroom. I lay you down on your back and remove your sandals, your pants and panties, pulling them down and off and dropping them to the floor. I look over your legs and pussy with the calm, intense eyes of an animal about to mate. Our eyes meet, and you nod, exposed and helpless and ready.

CHAPTER 31

Washcloth

You feel my hands on your ass cheeks and the push away as I unsheathe the length of my cock from your ass with a satisfied grunt. You get a queasy feeling in your tight stomach as you feel your abused asshole struggling to close. A hand comes down and grips the center of the chain between your tits. Your mind whispers, *Oh God, no, wait,* as my fist and the chain rise up and the slack in the chain disappears. Both of your breasts are stretched tight, and the pull doesn't stop. You cry out and get yourself awkwardly to your hands and then kneeling straight up. The chain stops for a moment and then pulls. You turn with it and go down to your hands, barely managing to start crawling as your breasts are tugged hard out ahead and pulled straight. Your mind flashes on your nipples coming off with the clamps and the chain dragging away. You begin to crawl with effort, with the pull, and you are led behind me to the bathroom, head down. You hear the turn of the faucet knob and the shower going on. Your chain is tugged, and you look up to see me standing in the stall, holding a washcloth in my hand, low and close to your face.

"My cock has been in your dirty ass."

You look at the washcloth. You look at the shaft and head of a cock inches from your face and then back at the sudsy washcloth in my hand. Your breasts are on fire and your nipples icy numb with needle-hot pain. Your pussy is a dripping, thrumming powder keg about to explode from a touch, a graze, anything, a good hard fucking. Your pussy spasms painfully as you reach for the cloth.

You pause for just a moment as your composure weakens, and you fight yourself to regain it. You feel your lower lip trembling, your fingertips touching the cloth now, and your pussy on edge, right on the edge—fat and bloated, needing to cum so badly, you can hardly think, hardly play. It's an effort to keep your hand on the cloth. You just want to reach down and frig your cunt. *You can watch me, sir; put on a show please, sir. Please let me lay down, let me do this. My pussy is—ooh, fuck, please.* You look up into my eyes with an embarrassed and apologetic you're-not-gonna-believe-how-bad-I-need-to-cum look on your face. Your lower lip moves. The silly, dead-serious hope is in your eyes, and the tensing, tiny hunches in your body. *Please let me cum, please, sir.*

I look down into your eyes, and you are sure I know what you are thinking. I'm so good at reading your mind, so good at that. *Please, sir, deal's a deal. You fuck my ass, and I get to cum. You gave me that, and I said yes. Please, no bullshit, please.*

My head gives a small back-and-forth, shaking *no,* and you feel the sting in your eyes. Your chest tightens, and you can't believe it. You want to cry; you need to cry. Your pussy, oh God—face tight with held-back tears, you bring the sudsy cloth to the base of my throbbing cock and slide it slowly up to the head and then back down. I lean back against the wall of the shower and close my eyes, pleasured. It's just you and this cock now, and you have your chore to do, your pussy preorgasmic and desperate down between your legs.

Chapter 32

Robe

Coming out of the shower, towel around you, you look so fresh and beautiful and womanly, I stop and stare. You are going about your routine, and you notice me staring, giving me a quick, happy smile as you continue on. You go over to the walk-in closet and open the doors, touching several dresses as you consider. The big, white terrycloth towel flows comfortably and snugly on your beautiful body.

I walk over to you and lift my hands, stopping just behind you and placing my fingertips lightly on the bare soft skin of your shoulders. You pause, your hand staying on that dark-blue outfit for a moment before I feel your body move. You turn softly around to face me. You are the day and the life and the world to me. You look at me with those breathtaking eyes, and you are revealed to me. I'm so undeserving of this moment, my eyes mist, and there is the closet around us and the still air of clothes and shoes—but for me, there is only you. I reach up; I have to reach up. I touch your cheek, and you smile from somewhere deep inside you, floating us on the beam of the here and now, beckoning me as if I had any thought otherwise. We draw closer, drab reality fading away as your lips touch mine. I am my heart and my passions, dropping all pretense. I kiss you, hard and fully, my arms of their own need taking you into my world, safe and loved.

Our lips part, just barely; our faces are so close, your eyelashes touch mine as you look down then up again into my eyes. My hands go lightly to the towel, and it vanishes down to your feet. Your poise and calm, your breasts, so perfect, the dark of your nipples. My hands find your hips and gently lead you out of the closet as I step back, taking you in hungrily, every move and moment of you—your legs, your feet, small and soft on the carpet; your hands sudden and smooth on my neck, and the way you bring us together for a heartfelt kiss.

I lift you easily in my arms, returning your kiss even more as I get you to the bed. I lay you gently down, lying down between your legs, watching your eyes close and your hand touch your breast. I bring my mouth close and take in all of the soft petals at once, pressing on them with lips over teeth as you moan quietly. I bring my finger up and rub gently, feeling your leg muscles and the small shifts of your hips as I massage. I breathe in the scent of your juices rising in the slit, easing my finger away from the swelling lips and touching softly on the hood, touching so softly, I can feel the pulse of your clit down inside. I walk the tip of my tongue into your moistening slit as my fingertip plays casually, easing down the clit hood, politely insistent and curious. I close my mouth on your slit and suck for a moment, taking the sweet drops of juice I find there. You groan out loud as my tongue begins to trace up and down, the full length up and down. You whisper and groan again in total agreement as my fingertip finds your hardening clit and stays on the very top, the hard edge, riding it back and forth.

My tongue traces up and down, gliding now in your juices, your pussy responding and welcoming, opening around my tongue as I ease it in deep and go into wide, slow circles. Swiping around and against the sensitive walls, my fingertip works your stone-hard clit, smearing juices and working it. I watch your arms go out straight, your hands wave over and on the sheets before you press them down deliberately and arch your back. You flood my mouth with your juices as you buck hard from the orgasm wracking your body. You're gripping fistfuls of my hair as your knees lift and you coil into another orgasm, letting out a guttural groan of bliss and place. Stamping your feet flat on the mattress, you lift your hips and rock your spasming pussy on my face and fingers before you fall back on the pillow, spent. My arms come down to cradle you as you breathe hard into my neck.

Printed in the United States
By Bookmasters